I
Like
Being
Watched

-

Jessica Gadziala

Dedication

This one goes out to my readers who are
always willing to take a chance on something
new with me.
I appreciate you all more than you can know.

I
Like
Being
Watched

One

Wynn

"What do you mean there were cameras?" I asked, carefully cutting into the unicorn-colored bagel filled with confetti cake frosting—little pieces of flower-shaped sprinkles that were almost cheerful enough to give us both some hope.

We'd made a habit of eating fun, trendy treats when we got together. It made our otherwise underwhelming lives feel mildly more interesting.

Except for the pickle ice cream.

We don't talk about the pickle ice cream.

It was a bright but cold Tuesday morning—the kind of cool that sank into your skin, into your bones, no matter how many layers you piled on.

We were sitting in our favorite coffee shop with its farmhouse-chic decor—painted white hardwood floors with just enough scuffs from high heels and impatient children's sneakers to give it a little character and history, ship-lapped walls in a variety of different rustic stains, and mismatched tables and chairs—at our favorite spot near the window.

We waited an hour to get in, but in our opinion, it was worth the wait. We liked to park for a while, chase away the blues that came with the most useless day of the week, while being able to watch the foot traffic, window shopping off of moving mannequins because we both knew we couldn't afford to buy anything as frivolous as new wardrobe items when neither of us had chosen degrees that guaranteed financial freedom. We found ourselves both recently graduated with crippling student loan debts and very few prospects for paying them off without ending up in some soul-sucking dead-end type situation.

Perry had it worse than I did. What with her track record of never staying at any one job for longer than a few weeks and all. Though, if I were being honest, I was steadily catching up to her, finding that my dozen or so side gigs were simply not going to cut it long term. Hell, it wasn't really even cutting it now.

I loved my mother more than words for always encouraging me to follow my passions in life, but with the cold hand of grown-up responsibilities holding me in its unyielding grip, I was starting to wish she'd maybe told me that yeah, it was great for me to fiddle around with art in my free time, but that it would be wise to get a degree in accounting or law or freaking library sciences. Something, anything that made me any kind of money.

Bless her hippie heart.

Unlike her, I didn't have a stable, sensible sort of man who worshipped the ground I walked on, who happily let me fiddle around in my craft room while he lovingly took care of all the less fun parts of life.

Like paying the light bill that had started calling four times a day. And when they went past three, they were about a week away from blanketing your world in darkness. The fact that I knew this—and had a cheap candle collection at hand for the possibility—really just showed where I was existing, socio-economically speaking.

I was half-tempted to take pictures of my feet doing weird things and selling them to the foot fetishists on Instagram.

And I was only half-joking about that.

"I mean there were cameras. Like... everywhere."

Perry, well, she was one for dramatics. Which was fitting, since she had majored in it, spent her weekends clutching her chest in Shakespeare plays on off-off-off Broadway shows or screaming in D-horror movies made on a shoestring budget that made shaky-cam found footage films seem high quality.

To people like Perry, very little didn't require big eyes or stunned gasps or, well, very overblown embellishments.

"Everywhere... where?" I asked, figuring she simply meant on the perimeter of the house to deter criminals. Or mailmen from tossing your packages from the window without getting out of their little trucks.

"Well, there was one in the kitchen, the dining room, the den, the study, the billiard room, the conservatory..."

In case it wasn't clear already, Perry had been working in a small ecosystem that dared to call itself a single-family home. Twelve-thousand square feet for one full-time resident, one part-time resident, and a couple house workers who came and went on their own schedules. What one person could do with twelve-thousand square feet was beyond me since I struggled to fill up a very generous nine-hundred square foot apartment.

"You're sure they were cameras? Rich people have those little motion sensor things mounted in the corners of rooms to set off their alarms when they are not around," I reminded her.

"Oh, he has those too!" she told me, bright silver-blue eyes going big.

I really hoped she made it big someday. Or at least landed a steady gig on a popular TV show or something. It would be a real shame if more people didn't get to see her unique face full of sharp angles light up when she was speaking. I'd never met someone with such expressive eyes, or brows that seemed to have conversations all by themselves, or a mouth that pulled off a pout like I hadn't seen outside of old black

& white movies, or her long, shining black hair that was practically its own character on her very body.

"But there are cameras too. *Hidden* cameras."

"Not too well hidden if you found them."

"I used to work as a nanny. I know a hidden camera when I see them. And, you know, when you are literally solely responsible for the life of someone else's offspring, a hidden camera is expected. But what the heck does he need cameras for?"

"He's rich. Rich people have expensive things."

Perry, having grown up in the humblest of humble households, sometimes struggled understanding how the one-percent lived. And, really, who could understand the dick-measuring contest that was buying bigger and bigger yachts just to show up some other guy in the marina?

The rich were as incomprehensible to me as people who willingly gave up carbs.

"I guess. Maybe. I just didn't like it. It freaked me out. I mean, what if he was sitting in his fancy office in the city staring at me while I wiped down his kitchen counters? It was just creepy."

That right there was one way Perry and I differed.

She heard hidden cameras and men watching from behind screens and she thought freaky and creepy, got goosebumps down her arms and across the back of her neck.

I got goosebumps too.

But of a completely different kind.

The kind that positively shivered across my skin, that set my nerve endings up in cold flames, that sank in and warmed up as they moved through flesh and tendon and muscle, as they settled down into my very bones. Burning hot. A blazing inferno. Lighting my whole body on fire.

I'd briefly dated a psych major in my freshmen year who had decided to shrink me. In his case, shrink me down, though he liked to call it 'helping' me.

You're an exhibitionist, Wynnie.

One couldn't argue against that when there was clearly a lot of evidence to support the claim.

It's a disorder. It's a paraphilia.

One could say I was not a fan of being lumped in with pedophiles and people who wanted to fuck animals.

I drew a line in the sand at that. One where I was on one side and that asshole was on the other.

I mean, really, who was he to judge me on my fetish when he got off playing a stern teacher who whipped my ass with a ruler before jerking off on my tits?

People in glass houses shouldn't pull out their BDSM gear then call their furry neighbors 'freaks' at the block party.

I'd maybe gone ahead after that breakup—and a dozen or so drinks with Perry to celebrate my newfound singledom—and looked up my so-called 'disorder.'

It took about two pages before I decided it didn't apply to me. Since I had no childhood trauma or sexual abuse or even hyper-sexuality. I mean, I liked a good tour of the sheets as much as any other healthy, red-blooded, twenty-something, but it wasn't like I was rubbing one out every twenty minutes just to be able to think straight.

I just liked being watched.

I liked the power of that.

I got off on the idea of someone sitting there somewhere private and seeing me bend over, seeing my shirt spill open in the front, and getting off on me.

I liked it.

And I had as long as I could remember.

Way back to my high school days when I had left my curtains open so my next-door neighbor who was a grade higher than me could see me from his desk in front of the window as I slipped out of my clothes and walked around my room in nothing but a barely-there thong.

I could feel his eyes on me as I pretended to innocently move around my room, shifting objects here and there, checking my phone, dancing around to some music.

It had turned my body molten to see his hand slide under the desk, to see his arm jerking up and down.

It was my thing.

And I refused to be ashamed of it.

Even if it wasn't exactly common knowledge about me.

Perry didn't know. Because, well, when it came to sexual preferences, I was a bit old-school in that I thought that was the business of you and your sexual partners only. It was in the vault. Along with cock size and shameful personal confessions. I firmly believed the world would be a better place if more people respected the sanctity of the interpersonal vault.

"Perry, for that kind of money, I would let him sit in the room and watch me as I cooked him dinner bare-ass naked in high heels."

To that, her nose wrinkled up. "I mean, I am going to miss the money," she admitted. "But I stashed a lot of it away to hold me over while I look around. I think Sly's place is hiring."

Sly was her on-again-off-again boyfriend who thought rolling his own cigarettes made him cool, and claimed any music made after the nineties was complete and utter shit. I didn't care for Sly. And by 'didn't care for,' I meant that I had called him a 'useless, unfaithful, dickwad' to his face on more than one occasion. Yes, dickwad. I was bringing out the big guns for that particular animal. Aim, cock, shoot. Unfortunately, he seemed to have nine lives, and Perry loved each one of them.

"Would you be pissed at me if I applied for the position?" I asked, choosing my words carefully.

"Wynn, what if he is like... selling the footage?" she asked, literally placing a hand against her lips as though this was just an all-too-shocking idea.

"Well, at least I would feel like I'd been paid well for it. I mean... Per, I could really use that twenty-five an hour. I am drowning. I can handle a paranoid boss with a security fetish."

To that, her face sank, likely thinking about her own bills piling up on her kitchen counter. They were just going to keep coming. We both understood the grueling pace of this particular hamster wheel.

"I won't be pissed. Of course not. But, like, maybe bring some pepper spray with you to work if they hire you? I just don't like those cameras. They give me the heebie-jeebies."

They gave me the hot-and-bothereds, but I wasn't going to admit that. Even best friends were entitled to their secrets.

"Was it a pain in the ass to get the job?" I asked, even though I figured anyone could be a house manager if they, you know, knew how to manage their own household. How hard was it to make sure toilet paper was ordered before you ran out?

"No, I mean, I never even met with the owner. I talked to Elsbeth, who is the cook. I guess because she's been around for ages, they used her to do the first round of interviews. And from there, she moves you onto Blake. He's the younger brother to Fitzwilliam Buchanan."

When she spoke of him, she always used his full name. Fitzwilliam Buchanan. Like he was some big celebrity. From what I understood, he was just some investment banker guy who was born rich then managed to make himself even richer in the years since his father passed. Maybe that meant he deserved a respectful *Mr. Buchanan*. But I thought the whole name thing was a little silly. I mean, most people referred to *presidents* just by their surnames.

This man was no leader of the free world.

He was likely just your run-of-the-mill average old dude with silver hair and the silver spoon shoved up his ass to match.

"Was Blake as pretentious as his brother's name is?" I asked, reaching for my half-cold coffee, grimacing a little as the sugar-free caramel met my tastebuds. Hot, you barely even noticed the artificial flavor of the sugar-free stuff. Cold, though, it stripped everything down to their base notes. And sugar-free caramel's base flavor was, well, chemicals. I tried to convince myself it was a healthier choice to have since we were sharing the frosting bagel. All the while I knew I had a fresh bag of Cool Ranch off-brand Doritos waiting for me on the counter at home, daring to call itself my dinner.

"I think his name is kind of romantic. Like some hero from a bodice-ripper. But, no, Blake is actually nice. Charming."

Nice and charming.

Why she was dating Dickwad Sly and not Blake Buchanan was beyond me. It sure wasn't because Blake wouldn't have wanted her. All guys who liked the fairer sex liked her. It was a law of nature. The sun rose, boobs floated in a pool, and men liked Perry Pearlman.

Maybe Blake was blond.

Perry didn't like blonde.

She quipped it was why the two of us could never be together. That, and not, you know, the fact that both of us were straight.

"Did they need a physical, blood test, and the promise of your firstborn son?" I asked, scraping some frosting off the plate with a pad of my finger.

To that, she gave me one of her brilliant smiles—pearly whites that were somehow all hers without the aid of orthodontia or bleaching sessions at the dentist on full display.

"No, it was an easy interview. I mean, it wasn't like one of those stuffed-shirts interviews we did during our sophomore year." Back when we thought working at a temp agency would be a good way to make cash. Honestly, we'd probably done it because we liked the idea of getting to wear fancy outfits to 'the office' every week. But sitting at a desk all day, answering phones, filing, pretending to know how to draw up a spreadsheet, it all got old pretty quickly. "He mostly just asked questions about multitasking and what kind of manual labor you are willing to do or not."

"What? Did the job require laying bricks or something?"

"Just general cleaning. There is a cleaning service that comes in once a week to do the deep stuff, but, apparently, Fitzwilliam Buchanan is a bit of a neat freak or something. He wants everything swept and mopped, and the surfaces wiped. And, I mean, the only other duties include making sure everything in the house is stocked and that all the staff members are doing their jobs. It was actually kind of nice to be able to move around and actually get something done."

"I can't believe you are leaving such an easy gig."

"I draw the line at spying. Makes me feel all squirrelly. But if it doesn't bother you, then, yeah, it is a sweet job. You can listen to music or audiobooks all day and get paid to do it. Plus, it's a beautiful house. I took maybe like fifty selfies with the soaking tub in the background. My heart aches, knowing it is sitting there, never being used. It should be a crime."

"Do you have the original contact information?"

"Yeah, I'll send it all over. Just... be careful, you know?" she asked, standing, slipping into a massive infinity scarf that had to have taken up four or five skeins of yarn, in a bright mustard yellow color that worked on her and most definitely did *not* work on me, much to my complete disappointment.

"I'm always careful," I reminded her, slipping into my jacket, bringing our plate and cups over to the mess station.

When it came to friendship dynamics, Perry was the one always kind of following her heart into the oddest of places, often needing to call me to come pluck her up out of a shady situation.

While me, well, I was home using every second of spare time I could find, trying to get more of a following for my art online so that I could eventually make a living doing that.

It was hard, but not impossible. I saw artists strike it big every day. And it wasn't like I was trying to make a fortune or anything. I just wanted to make enough so that I could do it full-time. Or only have to have a very part-time job on the side.

"Text me if you get an interview," she demanded as we moved out onto the sidewalk, the late fall air biting at our heat-accustomed skin.

"Will do. Send me the details to your next show," I told her, smiling as she did a little happy wiggle. It didn't matter to her that it was a very small-time play written by a guy we'd gone to school with, she was as excited as she would be if she landed a leading role in *Phantom* on Broadway.

That was one of the reasons we had managed all the ups and downs of our college years and beyond. We were both incredibly passionate about our chosen professions. Even though they weren't giving us what we wanted. Yet.

Eternal optimists, despite the often crushing reality.

I had just set up a fresh canvas in my spare room that was too small to have the audacity to call itself a bedroom, but worked rather beautifully for a studio, when my phone rang, bringing with it the links from Perry.

Apparently, whoever posted the ad for help in the first place never bothered to take it down. Whether that was simply a lapse in judgment, or evidence of other people getting the job and getting creeped out about the cameras, and therefore perpetually leaving a position that needed to be filled, I had no idea. It worked in my favor, though, seeing as I couldn't exactly say where I heard about the job in the first place.

Ten minutes later, I had all the information filled out, turned off my phone, and got to work. I never got long between my odd jobs, so when I did have a little span of time, I disconnected from the world, wanting to be able to lose myself for whatever snippet of time I was able to.

I knew artists that got more inspired surrounded by hustle and bustle, who needed to blast music, who needed some other sort of stimuli to get in the zone. I envied them. I needed silence to focus. This was something I could likely blame my mother for. She believed art was a form of meditation. And anyone who ever got their *Om* on knew that silence was generally recommended or else your mind started to wander.

I figured art school would eventually rid me of finicky habits.

No such luck.

So I had no idea until three hours later while juggling four dog leashes—one belonging to the corkscrew-tailed, severely overweight (and happy about it, therefore completely disinterested in exercise of any sort) bulldog—that there had been a missed call on my phone.

"Shit shit shit. See, Hagrid," I grumbled at the bulldog who looked up at me blankly. "If I didn't have to drag you every step of this walk, I would have checked my phone sooner," I told him, reaching down to give his wide head a pat, something that usually motivated a couple more steps out of him.

I hit the play button, cradling my phone between my ear and shoulder, my heartbeat already skittering around. Some would call this nerves. Interviews of any sort had a way of doing that to you. But I knew better. I knew this feeling all the way back to when I'd casually left my blinds open in my dorm room knowing that the guy standing outside my first-level window was watching me as my hand slid down my body, as it started stoking a fire.

This was the anticipation of getting a chance to fulfill my need to be watched again. It had been so long that I was already fantasizing about what I might wear on my first day to work, what would be professional, but allow things to get a little heated should I find the right camera at the right time.

It wasn't where my head should have been, of course. I was practical—and broke—enough to know I couldn't screw around at work. Not really. I needed the money, which meant I needed to keep the job for a while.

I wasn't going to ruin it for myself.

But if I was supposed to be doing manual labor, I figured it wouldn't be outside the realm of possibilities that I might get hot and fan the air into my shirt, maybe accidentally lifting it a bit too high. Or reaching down to fix the vacuum cord into the little holders when my skirt was just a tad short.

Nothing crazy.

Nothing that would get me fired.

I was just going to tease the lines of propriety.

Just a little game.

Just something to give me a bit of a fix.

If he had cameras, he likely wanted a show.

Who better than me to give it to him?

Two

Wynn

My life was a series of hemming and hawing every single article of clothing I put on until seventy-five percent of my closet was strewn around my bedroom, and I inevitably circled right on back to my first choice to begin with, slipping it on, chiding myself for being so damn indecisive and such a chronic over-thinker.

If I added up how much time I wasted on this particular cycle, I would likely have the time I always lacked to get my hair and face in order.

I was rushing out the door with my mascara tube in my hand, swiping a lightly tinted balm to my lips as I said a little prayer that my hair would dry fully by the time I got to my appointment.

In the end, just as in the beginning, I had settled on a pair of basic black slacks I had bought for an occasional bartending gig I landed when a friend of mine needed an extra hand with her shift. They were hot and rode up in weird places, but I figured they were the most professional pair of bottoms I had in my closet. I paired the slacks with a simple deep hunter green long-sleeved, button-up blouse, leaving the top button open, but no more. And, lastly, I had on a pair of black ballet flats since I figured you didn't want to show up for a job interview that would involve some light labor dressed like you were seeking a corner office.

First impressions mattered.

I really wanted to make a good one.

Because one look at my bank account that morning while I ate off-brand cereal and questionable milk made me realize I had to get this job. I needed the money. Even if I managed to pull all my little side gigs and sell a painting or two this week, I would still be in the red.

I had to nail this.

So I had to look the part.

I lucked out being stuck behind a train for a few minutes, letting me get my lashes lacquered, inspecting my teeth, popping in a mint, and spritzing on my perfect work perfume—a light vanilla and rose scent that not a single person I'd ever come across had found offensive—then finally made my way across town.

Into, you know, the nice area of it.

Where every house was a sprawling estate that would likely cost a couple million very easily.

None of them, however, came anywhere close to the one I turned my car into.

The one with the custom paver driveway that likely set it back a cool couple hundred grand. The landscaping with its intricately shaped bushes and hedges likely cost a small fortune to maintain as well, along with the sprawling lawn that was likely bright green all summer, and the pristine, gleaming pool I could see a sliver of in a glass room attached to the back of the house.

All those people—gardeners, lawn service, pool guy—I would be in charge of managing.

It was a foreign concept but one that felt interesting and wholly doable.

I mean, I could walk six dogs at once. I could be a shot girl to a group of gross, horny old guys who wanted to do body shots off of me and licked a little more than they should have. I could babysit kids and help elderly people run their errands, and teach pissed off teenagers how to paint in their forced art therapy classes.

I could do *all* of that.

In the same week.

I could absolutely do this.

I parked my car, inwardly worried it might leak something onto the expensive driveway and that I might be expected to shell out money I didn't have to replace the pavers, took a deep breath, and made my way up toward the towering white stucco home.

As one might imagine, a multitude of massive windows gleamed in the late fall sunlight, reflecting back the barren trees, giving no insight onto what might lay inside.

But I would soon find out as I pressed my finger into the pad of the electronic doorknob. No sound accompanied it, and I wondered if I would ever be cool enough in life to own a doorbell that didn't chime through the whole house.

It wasn't long before the door pulled open, producing a woman in a utilitarian gray dress that cinched at the waist and came down to the kneecaps, worn by a woman closer to my grandmother's age than my mother's with black hair flecked with salt & pepper, bright brown eyes that seemed to look right through me and see all my secrets, and a crucifix around her neck.

"You're Wynn," she said, giving me a nod.

"Yes. You're Elsbeth?"

"Yes. Come through. I have an appointment. I can only be with you for a few moments."

A few moments?

I had to convince this woman I was worthy of twenty-five dollars an hour in just a few moments? Perry? Sure. She could do that any day of the week, a natural-born chameleon with all the charm of your average, everyday, run-of-the-mill cult leader. Me, though, with my subpar social skills and strange resume full of various small gigs that never lasted very long? I wasn't so convinced.

But Elsbeth was already turning, heading inside, leaving me no choice but to follow behind.

The inside was what an episode of *The Lifestyles of the Rich & Famous* looked like, except more modern, sleeker. Gone were all the dark woods and stuffy Oriental rugs, replaced with sleek gray-washed hardwood floors, gray walls with minimalist, abstract art in neutral shades that I could have painted when I was two-years-old, but knew were likely purchased for the cost of a decent mid-sized SUV.

We walked past the butterfly staircase that led up to the second floor, and back into a kitchen that I was relatively certain was the size of my entire apartment with its stark white cabinetry, marble counters, and oversized, top-of-the-line stainless steel appliances. There was actually an echo in the space when Elsbeth spoke again.

"You can work the hours?" she asked, cutting to the chase. "Ten until seven. Monday through Thursday. Then ten until three on Friday. Mr. Buchanan takes half days on Fridays, and he likes his space."

Maybe so he could sit and watch his little home movies in private, I thought, a little tingle moving through me at the idea.

"Absolutely. My schedule is open." Or, rather, it would be if I got this job and informed all my other side gigs of the new arrangement. I might even try to squeeze them in on Friday afternoons and on the weekend. It was always good not to put all your eggs in one basket, my level-headed stepfather had told me after my mother urged me to go on a three-thousand-dollar artist retreat for a month as though I didn't have bills to pay. I loved her. And my heart ached that I couldn't go. But real life required at least a small amount of practicality.

"Good. That's good. And you can do the cleaning? It isn't much. Mr. Buchanan is naturally neat. But the mirror and counters and toilets all need a daily wiping down. That sort of thing."

"Of course."

"And you will need to go to the store for groceries. I will leave that list. As well as the dry cleaners or any other errand you find written down for you. I saw you have your own car, so that is good. You can submit receipts for gas to Mr. Buchanan at the end of the month. And communication skills are important. To make sure the groundskeepers and pool cleaners, anyone doing any sort of work here is doing what they are meant to be doing, not lazing about."

My lips curved up slightly at that. "I can be a good motivator when the occasion calls for it," I told her. "I might even enjoy it."

"Good. That's good," she agreed, sharing my smile. "Okay. I will pass you on to Blake. He prefers being called Blake. Says Mr. Buchanan is his brother. He should be here in a moment. He was taking a call in the study. I have to get going. It was nice meeting you, Wynn," she told me, already grabbing her purse and rushing out the door.

The kitchen was spotless.

Curious, I walked over to the fridge, opening it, seeing a dozen or so glass containers full of various items. Slices of salmon with a side of asparagus and some rice in some, brightly colored vegetable and beef stir fries in others. There were salad greens and a massive green smoothie. Nothing even resembling unhealthy. I mean, the man's only condiments were mustard, hot sauce, and some kind of homemade salad dressing that looked like little more than oil, vinegar, and some spices floating around.

"It's sad, isn't it?" a male voice asked behind me, making me jump, cringing at myself for getting caught snooping.

"I'm sorry. I shouldn't have looked. I was just curious since Elsbeth left but there was no evidence that she'd cooked."

Blake Buchanan was somewhere in his mid-twenties, brown-haired, blue-eyed, dressed in jeans and a button-up. Young, confident, rich, but not snooty.

"Fitz likes having meal prep instead of daily cooking. I guess so he has some choice in what he is eating. Even though it all looks entirely too healthy to me. Unclench your hands, Wynn, I'm not going to tattle on you for looking. If you get the job, you will be looking at every inch of this house. I'm Blake. And this is really just a formality. Elsbeth usually weeds out the lunatics. I just make sure whoever she picks isn't too senile to get the job done."

Or too old to be hot enough for the cameras, I imagined, though I wondered if he knew about them, if he helped his older brother indulge in his little fantasies. Maybe Blake was just given the instruction to pick someone young and reasonably attractive, with no explanation as to why.

"I only spent two minutes with her, but she seems like a tough cookie."

"That she is. She once slapped me across the hand with a wooden spoon when I tried to sample something she was making," he told me, smiling.

I wondered if Elsbeth knew about the cameras, if she cared.

"Well, you should have known better," I teased, getting another of those charming smiles of his.

"So, Wynn. What do you do for a living?"

"Excuse me?"

"Well, no one does this job because they are a house manager. We had a musician, a children's book illustrator, a cosplayer—and, yes, she took that very seriously in her spare time—, and I think the most recent was an actress of some sort."

"May I ask why there have been so many?"

"Oh, this and that. The musician got a gig on a small tour. The illustrator moved back home with her ailing parents. The cosplayer got pregnant and didn't want to do any of the cleaning. And the actress, well, her I am not sure about. She just up and quit. Maybe she was just flighty like that."

To be fair, she was.

And the fact that everyone else left the job because of some other kind of life event made any of the small worries I might have had about the position slip away. Perry likely was being—as was very on-brand for her—dramatic about the cameras. They probably were simply situated where there were valuables or around exits of various kinds, Mr. Buchanan wanting to keep an eye on his pricey possessions.

He might only view the footage as a security measure, but he was going to be pleasantly surprised by what he would find once I got the position.

And just like that, ten minutes later, I had all the forms filled out, was walking down the front path with a small binder full of household information—preferences about brands and scents that were acceptable or banned from the household, the names and locations of shops and dry cleaners—when a sleek black Lamborghini hummed up the drive, making me gasp and jump to the side as it nearly side-swiped me to get into its chosen space, which so happened to be beside mine.

The engine cut.

The door opened.

And out slid the most gorgeous man I had ever seen outside of a television screen.

Yes, he was primetime TV hot.

Maybe even late-night Showtime hot.

Standing at least around six-three, his body was strong, yet not overly jacked—a swimmer's body, one might call it, long and lean, wide of shoulder, but narrower at the waist and hip.

He had sharp slashes for cheekbones that created small hallows beneath. Under what could only be called a stern brow were striking eyes the color of morning skies illuminated with fresh light, so bright they almost hurt to look at, all the while begging you never to look away. They were made all the more dramatic by the rich, thick black lashes that nearly matched his dark brown hair. His jaw was a severe angle, so chiseled it looked as though it could slice your finger if you trailed it along that edge.

Generally speaking, my desire to be watched had nothing at all to do with the attractiveness of the man doing the watching. It wasn't about me being attracted to them, but rather their desire for me that seemed to fuel the behavior.

That said, there was no mistaking the thrill inside I felt, knowing a man who was that beautiful was going to sit down to rewind his security footage only to get something he hadn't bargained for, that it would make his cock stiffen, would make him reach up to undo a shirt button, would have him reaching under his desk to relieve the pressure that came with his need for release.

I could feel my own desire growing as he looked over, his head jerking back a bit at seeing me standing there, like he had missed me in the driveway, hadn't noticed almost hitting me.

"Mr. Buchanan," I greeted him, giving him a smile, wondering if my need was as plain on my face as it felt in my body, that frantic sizzling and simmering in my belly, in my core.

"Who the hell are you?" he asked, his voice a deep, rich, smooth sound that washed over my skin, leaving goosebumps in its wake.

"Wynn," I told him, not minding a bit when his gaze did a sweep of my body before landing on my face again. "Your new house manager," I clarified.

His reaction was slow at first.

He stared at me for a long second.

Then away over the front lawn.

Then back at me.

"Shit," he hissed, slamming his car door, and making his way up the front path, leaving me looking after him until he disappeared.

Taking a breath, I climbed in my car, flipping down the visor, looking at my reflection. Blonde hair, red lips, green eyes, but they were heavy-lidded with desire. And my usually pale cheeks were tinted pink with it as well.

I turned over my car, carefully backing out of the driveway, making sure not to let a tire touch the mostly dead but very uniformed grass, pausing at the end to let a sleek silver sedan pass.

My gaze slid back to the house, finding the drapes parted in the front room, one I had gotten a short glimpse of while rushing to keep up with Elsbeth.

The study.

And there he was.

Fitzwilliam Buchanan.

Tall, dark, handsome, looming.

And completely unprepared for what I had in store for him.

Three

Fitz

She was too fucking pretty.

I was going to kill Blake.

Sure, I had given him the directive to make sure Elsbeth chose candidates who were young and spry enough to handle all the housework and errand-running. But I meant someone under sixty, since she'd once tried to have her own only partially mobile great aunt take the position.

My brother, notoriously self-involved and lacking anything even akin to a sensible bone in his body, somehow heard this as 'find me the youngest and most attractive women this country has to offer, and stick them in front of me five days a week.'

Maybe it was simply him misunderstanding an order. It wouldn't be the first—or last—time.

But a part of me was convinced he was doing it deliberately.

Why, was the question I needed answered, though.

"Blake!" I called, knowing the sound carried to damn near every corner of the first floor where he would be lurking, making some sugar cereal for himself as though he was a five-year-old instead of a grown-ass man. "Get your ass in here," I demanded, hearing shuffling of feet a moment before he moved into the doorway, giving me a smile.

"You rang?"

"What the fuck do you think you're doing?"

"Well, I was trying to find something to eat."

"You know what I mean. The girl. What are you doing?"

"Hiring your house manager. Like I was assigned to do, boss." It bothered Blake, whether he would admit it or not, that I was the one who held the purse strings of the family fortune. I even had control over how much of his trust was released to him and when. Not because I was a controlling asshole—though Blake would certainly make that argument—but because our father had been wise enough to know that his younger son went through money like water, and would squander away any large sum given to him in under a year, leaving him destitute for the rest of his life.

He worked for me because I felt a familial obligation. He handled hiring and firing of my house manager as well as a small-time job at the office, doing things that couldn't end up making the company look bad because of his poor work ethic.

He lived in the pool house in the backyard—a structure big enough to comfortably house a family of four—but he spent a lot of his time in my house, finding ways to piss me off because he felt entitled to do so.

The charm he had naturally fooled most people. But not me.

I knew the whiny, spoiled brat underneath, one who never developed the work ethic our father had possessed, that he had passed on to me.

That said, he was my brother. I loved him, even with the flaws, even with the constant headache he gave me. I was hoping that by being near me for a while, some of my hard working attributes would rub off, and he could eventually get more serious about his life and future. He had it in him. He just chose to take the immature route instead.

I was starting to wonder if maybe he always would.

"Is there any particular reason they have all been pretty twenty-somethings?"

"A little eye candy never hurt anyone. Besides, you have to like this one. She's just your type."

Yeah, that was the problem.

I worked too much, barely ever had time for sleep, let alone going out and finding a woman. Then having the real-life equivalent of my dream woman showing up in my damn house? That was a problem. I usually had a lot of control, but I wasn't one-hundred-percent sure I wouldn't pounce on the woman if she was willing, becoming that prick who makes someone's work-life an uncomfortable place to be.

"And why would I want someone who was my type managing my house?"

"You need to get laid, big bro," he declared.

"This might be news to you, but you don't fuck women who work for you."

"Well, she's hired. So you will just have to deal with it now," he declared, shrugging, walking out of the room.

I wanted to call him back, to argue about it, but the larger part of me knew that it was useless, it never got us anywhere. He never changed, and I would just be pissed off after.

He was right about one thing, though.

This new woman was hired.

And I was going to need to deal with it now.

It shouldn't be that big of a problem.

None of the others ever were.

Of course, I had no idea at the time what Wynn Downey had in store for me...

Four

Wynn

I was trying not to screw it up.

That was what I had told my reflection as I carefully dressed for my first day of work.

Sure, a big part of me wanted to slip on a miniskirt, heels, and a tight, low-cut tank. But the rational part of me chose a simple white button-up with the top button undone, with a pretty blush lace bra underneath, and a demure-length skirt.

I needed the job.

I needed to appear professional.

Especially at first.

I mean, no one could blame me if I had to lean over to pick up something off the floor and my very professional shirt just slipped open a little in front of a camera.

So that was the plan.

Test the waters, get a little thrill, but make sure everything was above any sort of reproach. I needed the money. And I was actually kind of excited to take on a steady job.

I knew a lot of creative sorts who thought nine-to-five jobs cramped their vibe, but I had personally found that nothing made for worse art from me than financial upheaval. Constantly worrying how I was going to be able to cover an upcoming bill always took me right out of the mindset I needed to really escape into my work.

I was hoping a steady—and generous—paycheck would help spark a new fervor, the kind I had known in the early days of my college career, back when my lovely step-father so generously helped pay my bills so that I could get a leg-up in life. Those were the times when I would set up my supplies across my side of the dorm room, then set to work early in the morning, only seeming to come out of my trancelike state sometime after dark, arms aching, stomach grumbling, but with epic, beautiful pieces of art to show for it.

I'd even sold all those pieces.

Now?

I hadn't sold anything for months, not even the marked down canvases that my local coffee shops and libraries had posted up for me.

So I was going to be the best damn house manager anyone had ever seen. Who sometimes bent over in front of a camera or spilled out of her shirt. But since I was alone when it happened, no one could fault me for it.

Fitzwilliam Buchanan would have no idea there was any sort of agenda behind any of it. That was always what made it best, anyway, the man's belief that he had caught you in a private, exposed moment. It wasn't nearly as fun when they knew I knew they were watching.

Plan in place, I made my way to the Buchanan estate, pausing to roll my eyes at a concerned text from Perry before silencing my phone and tucking it into my purse that I stashed in a corner of the kitchen once Elsbeth let me inside.

From there, I was given my own key, a list of the household employees, and the expected daily and weekly duties before Elsbeth was shuffling off, leaving me alone in the sprawling mansion.

I hadn't gotten any sort of official tour, so notebook in hand, I made my way through the house, reminding myself that it wasn't snooping to get to know the place I would be working, that if I was supposed to clean the powder room on the first floor and the master bath on the second, then I certainly had a right to figure out where they were all situated.

The rest of the house was much like the main lower floor—an understated kind of classy, no fuss, no frills, everything in neutral grays or whites.

Except, it seemed, the master bedroom.

Fitzwilliam Buchanan was certainly a fan of the color black.

God, I was turning into Perry, using the man's whole name every time I thought of him.

The master bedroom was as massive as you might imagine with the square footage of the estate. But it was somehow dominated by a massive bed that seemed like it had to be custom made, larger than any king-sized I had ever seen, draped in black sheets, a black comforter, and black throw pillows.

The wall behind the bed was also painted a matte black, including all the built-in bookshelves that could be found there.

I mean this man was rich and anal enough about these sorts of things that even the books on the shelves had dust jackets printed up with matte black covers and shiny black titles and author names on the spine.

The drapes over the French doors that led onto the back balcony were drawn and, you guessed it, black.

The sheer amount of the one dark color should have made the space oppressive and gloomy. But even I—someone who loved color—found the space unexpectedly comforting and sleek.

I moved through the master bedroom, making my way into the bath, finding it in stark contrast to the bedroom, everything bright white much like the kitchen with its marble countertops and tile in the shower as well as the white soaking tub and the white walls.

"Strange," I decided, wondering what kind of man went from a dark bedroom to an almost painfully bright bathroom as I went into the drawers and cabinets, jotting down notes on brands of products, and how many were left of each thing.

It wasn't until I was making my way back into the bedroom that I saw it.

The first one I had noticed.

A camera.

I don't think anyone would have noticed it if they didn't know it was there. But there it was. A shiny circular spot in the spine of a book.

Adrenaline sizzled across my nerve endings as I forced my gaze away from it, not wanting it to be clear that I knew it was there, that it was watching me. That defeated the whole purpose.

Instead, I placed the notepad down on the nightstand as my gaze went to the bed, my hands reaching for pillows, fluffing them with perhaps more gusto than the task required, hard enough that my boobs burst open my second button by the time I got to the third pillow.

I finished the fluffing, then moved to the foot of the bed, grabbing the corners of the comforter while bending forward, feeling the cool air in the room brush over my partially exposed breasts as I shimmied the comforter straighter on the bed. Let's just say there was quite a bit of jiggle involved in this task. Necessary? Probably not. But I sure made it seem like a normal thing to do as my body heated, my sex clenching at the idea of Mr. Buchanan sitting down in his study after work, going over his security footage as I suspected any careful man would do the first day a new employee started in his home, and coming up on the footage of my tits spilling out of my bra and shirt, bouncing around as I made the bed he would later go to sleep in.

It was tame.

The whole thing was vanilla, all things said.

But it was just the right amount of excitement for me as I walked back to my notebook, picked it up, and walked innocently out of the room.

I went ahead and did another couple hours of tasks with the extra button open. Wiping surfaces, sweeping, restocking things from the massive storage closet between the kitchen and the garage.

It was only when I heard some of the men showing up to take care of the grounds that I ducked into the powder room, covered myself up, and made my way outside to greet them, introduce myself, and make sure everything was getting done.

It should have felt strange, running a house that didn't belong to me. Or running a house at all when all I'd ever needed to do was take care of my little apartment. And even that I, admittedly, did not do spectacularly. I mean I had once needed to use a coffee filter as TP when I had let myself run out.

But, suddenly, at this new job, I was finding myself on top of my game. I had lists upon lists upon lists. I actually brought my laptop to work on the third day to work on a spreadsheet that I pinned inside the door of the storage closet, making everything I needed to know right there when I needed to find it quickly.

Those first couple of days, I found a total of ten cameras hidden in various places. In the clock on the wall in the kitchen, behind a plant in the hallway, in the garage disguised as a lighter, in the living room inside a fragrance diffuser.

His study had multiple ones covering all corners of the room. One was inside a Bluetooth speaker, another as an extra carbon monoxide detector. I didn't see the third one for a long time. In fact, I was on my hands and knees, bending forward to reach for my pen that I'd *accidentally* had roll under the leather sofa, giving the other two cameras good angles—one looking down my parted shirt, noticing I had forgone a bra that day, the other hopefully catching my skirt riding up, showing off the bright red lace thong I'd put on that morning—and that was when I saw a little hole in the charging block plugged into the wall, something that didn't belong there, something that I knew from doing a little online research on the subject, was a hidden camera.

The man was paranoid, I had decided already, not a creep.

He had cameras in places that wouldn't normally catch people in compromising positions. There weren't, for example, cameras in any of the main bathrooms or guest bathrooms. But there was one in his own bathroom, hidden in the electrical outlet. Which was strange, sure, but not exactly creepy since he was a single man, and the only person who appeared to use that bathroom was himself.

So everything simply pointed to him being extremely security conscious.

Which was fine.

I didn't particularly care about the cause of the cameras, just their presence, just my ability to put on a show for them.

A show for him.

But after a solid week of no long glances when we passed in a hall, no eye-fucking me when he thought I wasn't looking, I was starting to wonder if he never viewed his footage after all.

Five

Fitz

You would almost think she was doing it on purpose.

That was how often one of the cameras caught her bent over just the right way, or her skirt slipping up when she reached over her head.

It was constant.

Daily.

More than a few times a day.

But, of course, she couldn't have been doing it on purpose.

That made no sense.

She was just a woman doing a job.

Sure, after the fourth straight day of wardrobe malfunctions, I perhaps thought she should decide to stop wearing button-up shirts, but that didn't mean there was anything untoward going on.

All that said, she was fucking killing me.

I had my reasons for the cameras. I didn't just set and forget them. Every night as I ate my dinner, I scanned through them quickly.

Well, I used to scan through them quickly.

Now?

Now, I sat down only after I was finished with dinner, a glass of whiskey at my side, with the house empty and quiet.

I set the fucking scene every night. Which ended up making me feel like a creep. But that didn't stop me as I went room to room as Wynn did, watching as she somehow managed to be exceptionally efficient and ball-achingly provocative at the same time.

Who looked sexy when wiping off a bookshelf?

Apparently, Wynn did.

And those breasts of hers seemed to have a mind of their own, breaking free from every single top she put on.

Sometimes, the woman didn't even have a bra on, her dusty pink nipples on full display while she continued to go about her job, seemingly oblivious to being exposed. How, I don't know. But nothing about her behavior implied she was intentionally exposing her chest or bending over and putting her whole ass on display for one of the cameras.

When I passed her in the hall, she was pure innocence, completely professional.

It was always *Mr. Buchanan* this. And *Mr. Buchanan* that.

I should have fired her the first time I watched one of those feeds of the security footage and my cock hardened, demanded attention, relief.

It was a recipe for disaster that I found myself horny as a fucking teenager for a woman who was working for me.

That said, it wasn't her fault.

And I would feel like an asshole firing her for something that she had nothing to do with. She was doing her job. And, admittedly, she was probably the best house manager I'd had over the years. I never had to leave a note about something running out or some errand not being handled. The pool was cleaner than it had ever been. The leaves that had been scattered on the driveway that seemed to always be there for a week before someone handled them, were gone by the time I got home in the evening, and never showed up again.

That old saying about good help being hard to find was true. In my experience, most of my house managers did the absolute bare minimum they could and still get paid. The musician used to bring her guitar and do live videos on social media for good chunks while on the clock. The illustrator spent at least an hour sitting at my desk doodling on her sketch pad. That last one—the actress—was constantly taking selfies in various spots in the house.

But whenever Wynn was around, she was doing something. Dusting, sweeping, mopping, cleaning bathrooms, reorganizing the pantry and the closets, going to the store, coming back and unpacking. She was busy from the moment she arrived until I got home, when she seemed to come out of her work fog. Maybe because she was interrupted. Most days, she was on her own save for the days when Elsbeth was around, bustling in the kitchen. On those days, Wynn got out of Elsbeth's hair, going to clean the upstairs instead. She seemed to thrive on her own, got in the zone, and handled shit.

I appreciated that.

It was a rare quality these days.

I would know. I had a hundred employees in my main office building. And most of them needed to be babysat, needed their hands held, needed constant motivation, were not self-starters. There were always a handful of team members who carried most of the weight. Adult professional life was like a constant high school group project. One person was there to create more problems. One was there to dick around and frustrate everyone else. One really never showed up. And then one? One did all the work, got the A for everyone else.

I tried, at work, to reward those who handled it all.

So to fire one in my home when they did so as well was asinine.

I should have just stopped watching, fast forwarded through the scenes that got hot. I couldn't seem to muster that sort of self-control, though.

It was a ritual every night.

"Mr. Buchanan," Wynn said, pulling me out of my swirling thoughts. I was supposed to be focusing on the report in front of me. I wasn't sure a single word of it had sunk in.

"Yeah?" I asked, raking a hand through my hair as a sigh escaped me.

"Can I get you something to eat?" she asked, surprising me. "You've been in here for over two hours," she added in that honey-sweet voice of hers.

"If that is the case, why are you still here?" I asked, glancing over at the clock. Sure, I left my office early on Fridays, but that didn't mean the work stopped there. And it always meant that the staff cleared out early to give me my privacy.

"The crew that is glazing the garage floor are taking longer than they said they would. Something about humidity levels," she said, rolling her eyes like she wasn't buying it. "It's not a big deal. I have nothing else going on. I want to make sure they do a good job. You're paying a small fortune for it," she added.

I wouldn't have even noticed the money being gone.

But I would have noticed the job not being done right.

So I appreciated her keeping an eye on them. I had completely forgotten they were even coming that evening.

"Ah, yes. Food."

"Which disgustingly healthy thing do you want tonight? Plain rice and an unseasoned chicken breast?" she asked, lips curving upward, teasing.

"You have a problem with healthy food?" I asked, brow lifting, wondering how she kept in shape if she didn't eat healthy herself.

"No. I enjoy a good salad as much as the next person. But you have to have a little variety in life. Cheese once a month never killed anyone, you know."

Eating healthy meant that I didn't have to work as hard in the gym to stay fit. But if I were being honest, eating had long since become something rote. Like brushing my teeth. Like flossing. Something necessary, but not overly enjoyable.

"Alright. How about you order pizza then? We can both use something to eat."

What the fuck was that?

I didn't eat dinner with my employees.

It blurred lines.

It made it harder to terminate them if the situation called for it when you shared a meal while discussing personal details.

"You want me to order pizza?" she asked, brows pinched like this news made no sense.

"That's what I said."

"What kind of pizza?"

"Doesn't matter."

"It doesn't matter? Are you sure? Because people put sardines on pizza. They put *baked beans* on pizza."

"In that case, cheese. Or pepperoni. Nothing crazy."

"Alright. Got it. From the petty cash?" she asked, reaching to pull a small notebook out of her back pocket. I imagined she kept a tally in there as she used money on errands. I had no doubt that there would be a spreadsheet with receipts attached on my desk when the cash was gone.

"I'll handle it. Go take a break for a bit."

She offered me a smile I struggled to interpret. Something relieved yet somehow excited at the same time.

"Okay. Thank you, Mr. Buchanan."

With that, she turned to walk off, that perfect ass of hers distracting me until she was out of view, going back toward the den, from the sound of her footsteps.

It was wrong.

God, it was so fucking wrong.

But my hand moved to the screen on my computer, clicking through my cameras, finding the one for the den, and blowing it up to overtake the screen.

There Wynn was, running her fingertips across the back of the dark brown material of the couch as she reached up with her other hand, pulling her hair free, shaking it around her shoulders. I swear it happened in slow motion, almost as if she was purposely making the move look as sexual as possible.

That was absurd, of course. She was alone. There was no reason to make something seem sexy when on your own.

So she was simply that hot all the time.

I didn't need to know that.

I was having a hard enough time keeping sane with her in my house.

She lowered herself down on the couch, giving me her profile as she pulled out her phone, searched around for a moment for—I imagined—a pizza place in the area, then dialing. I could hear the sounds of her voice, but not the words, not wanting to turn the volume up in case she might hear the echo of her voice from my study.

She hung up, slipping out of her shoes, softly rolling her neck before turning, lifting her legs up, lowering herself back on the couch, her legs facing the camera.

One of her arms lifted, her forearm resting on her forehead, her eyes going half-closed as her other hand rested on her stomach for a moment.

Before shifting downward.

Fuck.

Downward.

Over the top of her thigh.

Her fingertips traced the hem of her skirt.

My breath felt caught in my chest as I waited, sure it was going to end there, but also hopeful it wouldn't.

Then her fingers slipped her skirt upward, over her thigh, bunching it up near her hips, exposing a red lacy thong.

One of her legs lifted, went at an angle, foot planted on the cushion.

And then her hand slipped between her thighs, stroked up the crease of her thigh, then over the top of her panties before slipping under.

"Fuck," I hissed, my cock already hard, throbbing, begging for release.

My finger slipped to the volume button, sliding it upward, needing to hear her, catching the end of a small gasping sound as her finger slid over her pussy.

It was insane and inappropriate, but my hand slid down, undoing my belt, my button and zipper. As her fingers started working circles around her clit, my hand grasped my cock, pulling it out, stroking.

Through the speakers, her ragged breath was getting drowned out by soft, mewling noises as her chest started to rise and fall more quickly.

Her hand shifted, fingers slipping downward.

Her back arched as she let out a throaty moan as her fingers slipped inside her pussy.

I damn near came right then and there.

"*Ohhh... yes*," she whimpered, her hips rocking to meet the thrusts of her fingers as her other hand moved upward over her belly, sliding each button loose.

I swear each inch of exposed flesh was like a stab of need to my system before, finally, the last button was undone, and the sides slipped open, her bare breasts spilling out.

"Fuck," I hissed, stroking my cock harder, faster, as Wynn's hand closed over her breast, squeezing for a second before releasing. Her fingers moved to her nipple, tracing over it until it formed a hardened point, then rolling it between her thumb and forefinger for a long moment. "Pinch it," I murmured to myself, needing more. But it was almost as if she heard the demand because she grabbed her nipple, pinching, pulling, until she arched up off the couch with a deep, ragged moan.

I slid the volume a little higher so I could lean back in my chair and still hear her hitched breathing, her soft whimpers, her moans.

I watched as she slid another finger into her panties. And, judging by the way she spread her thighs a little wider, and the way her hips rose upward, that she slipped that third finger inside of her dripping pussy.

What was she thinking about as she finger-fucked herself?

Was she just lost in the sensations?

Or was she imagining someone's cock buried deep inside her, driving her up toward an orgasm?

Could she have possibly been thinking about my cock?

Why else would she feel the sudden need to fuck herself in my den after speaking to me?

A pathetic, needy part of me wanted her to be thinking about my thick cock deep inside her, stretching her, making her mine as she moaned and cried out, as her walls got tighter and tighter until...

"*Fuck*," I groaned as Wynn's orgasm slammed through her system, making her legs shake, and making her cry out loudly, too far gone to even care if she'd been heard.

She'd been heard alright.

And she'd brought me with her as she came, leaving me hissing and panting and completely spent after.

For all of two long minutes before I realized I came all over my fucking self.

Like some inexperienced incel.

"Christ," I hissed, grabbing for some tissues as I stood up.

I had to get upstairs before she came back out of the den. I had to clean myself up. And get myself together.

What the fuck was wrong with me?

I never reacted like that to a woman.

And I was damn sure never a fucking creep, jerking off to a woman who didn't know I was watching her.

I needed to get a hold of myself.

I had to stop watching Wynn.

I LIKE BEING WATCHED

Six

Wynn

It was an interesting turn of events to find myself watching him.

See, I'd heard him going upstairs, his steps hard and purposeful.

Like he hadn't seen me.

More than a little disappointed, I'd gotten off the couch to go back into the office.

To snoop.

I didn't even want to admit it to myself, but I wanted to snoop to see if he'd somehow missed me.

I hadn't exactly been quiet, for God's sake. I'd practically screamed out my orgasm, the one that was made so intense at the thought of him watching me, of his cock hardening in his pants because of me—aching and intolerable.

Moving behind his desk, I found his laptop still open.

And the image of the now-empty den on the screen.

Oh, he'd watched me alright.

And judging by the turned over tissue box on the desk, he'd done more than just felt achy and needy.

He'd jerked off while watching me please myself.

The jolt of pleasure was immediate and undeniable.

What I did next, though, was not.

I liked to be watched.

I didn't like to *do* the watching.

Yet there was no way I could deny that my hand slid to his laptop, switching through the cameras in his bedroom, then his bath.

And that was where I found him, standing with a confused and hard look on his face as he worked the knot off of his tie, tossing it into the hamper. Next, his fingers went to his shirt.

God, those fingers.

I'd thought about them rolling over my clit, sliding inside my body, as I'd touched myself in the den.

He had nice hands.

It wasn't something I usually noticed about a man, but I'd noted it several times when I was looking at him.

Big, masculine hands with neat fingernails. The perfect hands for finger-fucking a woman.

I'd never seen the man in anything but his perfectly tailored suits. Once, I thought I caught the flash of him coming back from the gym in basketball pants and a tee, but I couldn't say for sure.

I had no idea what was underneath.

Even if I had thought about it, I probably wouldn't have done him justice.

See, when you think of descriptions like "swimmer's body," you inevitably think thin of waist, wide of shoulder, and lean.

But sometimes you forgot that it took a lot of strength to swim well.

I certainly had forgotten that.

Because under Fitzwilliam Buchanan's suit was a whole lot of strength.

The man could have invented the term "washboard abs." None of the muscles were too bulky, but you could see the outline of a perfect eight-pack. And the dips. Good God, the man had those deep lower hip indentations that made your eyes want to follow them down, see where they led.

My eyes?

They were greedy.

So when his fingers undid his pants and boxer briefs, my gaze slid down the indented muscles of his Adonis Belt, finding the thick length of him.

That was another department my imagination wouldn't have done him justice in.

Below his cock were thick, strong thighs, the ones that wouldn't get tired if you wanted to go all night long. The arms, too, were strong and corded, and could more than readily handle as many push-ups as necessary, if you get what I'm saying.

The man was the definition of perfect.

Enough so that I was starting to think maybe it wouldn't hurt me to learn to like plain rice and bland, boring chicken a couple nights a week.

It did the body good.

He was proof of that.

"Oh, damn," I murmured to myself as he turned away from the camera, giving me a view not only of his wide, strong back, but the perfect, rounded, muscular ass of his too.

My desire, so recently sated by the orgasm in the den, hummed to life again as I watched Fitzwilliam Buchanan walk across his bathroom and into his shower where the water burst to life.

I knew his water.

It took a while to get hot. Long pipes for a massive house and all that.

So I knew it was bracingly cold as he stepped under the spray and let it wash over his body.

A thrill moved through me as I realized he wanted the cold shower. Because he'd been so worked up from watching me in the den that he'd jerked off and came all over himself like it was his first time.

He leaned forward, resting his forearm on the marble wall, then his forehead on his arm, just letting the cold water cascade over his body.

I thought I'd been drunk on power in the past, completely shit-faced by the way I could have a man's gaze guiltily watch me when he thought I didn't know, but knowing I brought a man like Fitzwilliam Buchanan to this place of complete overwhelm, this was a drug of a whole new caliber.

I was high off of it.

I was instantly addicted to it.

I needed more of it.

A small, niggling little voice whispered that I might never get enough of it.

So, I watched.

As he soaped up and rinsed off, as he dried off with the giant bath blankets he kept in all his bathrooms, and then I watched as he slipped into another almost identical pair of slacks and dress shirt that he'd left on the counter. He skipped the jacket.

And it was right about then that the doorbell rang.

I was so startled, I pushed away from the desk, knocking the chair into the wall.

I watched the laptop as my boss stiffened too, as realization dawned on him, making him fetch his wallet off of the nightstand.

"I'm coming," he called, even as I watched him rush out of the bathroom.

Things started to register then.

The pizza.

The pizza man at the door.

"Shit," I hissed, hopping up.

I just barely got the seat pushed back when he was reaching the lower landing of the staircase. Heart slamming in my chest, I rushed out from behind the desk.

Just in time.

"Oh," Fitzwilliam said, jolting. "Pizza," he added, brows pinching as he looked at me.

"I'm starved," I said, pretending there wasn't a husky edge to my voice as I said it.

Fitzwilliam's head shook a bit before he made his way to the door. I moved into the doorway in time to see him hand the delivery boy a fifty, and tell him to keep the change before closing the door.

"What?" he asked, seeing the look I knew I must have been giving him.

"I had a brief stint as a delivery driver in college," I told him, following him into the kitchen. "If I got a tip like that now and again instead of sexual innuendos and spare change, it might have been a longer-lived job."

"What did you go to college for?" he asked, reaching for a set of his fancy black stoneware plates with the gold edging and the tiny white speckles.

"Societal disappointment," I said. Then, to his confused face, I added, "Art major."

"Ah, I see," he said, a ghost of a smile on his lips.

"Blake says you tend to employ those like me."

"Like you? No."

God, he sounded so serious, so severe when he said that.

"I mean people like me. With less... useful passions in life. I think Blake said a cosplayer and an illustrator and an actress, among others."

"Which I believe says more about my brother's subpar selections than about their passions in life," Fitz said, sliding a slice of pizza onto my plate. "What do you do? Paint? Or draw? Sculpt?" he asked, eyeing his own slice a bit dubiously.

"I paint," I told him. "It's not going to bite, you know," I told him, catching a smirk toying at his lips.

"I'm working myself up to it," he claimed, putting down the plate, and going toward his wine rack instead. "Red?" he asked.

I shouldn't drink on the job.

I damn sure shouldn't drink on the job with a man whose cock I'd just been admiring not ten minutes before.

"Sure," I agreed, watching him check a few labels before deciding on one.

The last guy I'd dated thought beer in bottles was "fancy." So it was surprisingly appealing to watch a man who clearly knew a thing or two about the finer things in life carefully select a bottle of wine for you to share.

"Good?" he asked after handing me a long-stemmed glass.

"It doesn't taste like the watered-down rubbing alcohol taste that my three-dollar wine does, so yes," I told him, mentally making a note to replace the bottle the following workday. "Come on. I tried your wine. You try the pizza."

"I've had pizza," he insisted, moving back toward his plate.

"When?"

"It was a staple in college. Back when I didn't need to workout to stay fit," he told me, folding his slice, then taking a bite.

There was a low groan that escaped him that moved through my chest, then slid lower.

"Better than rice and unseasoned chicken, huh?" I teased, taking a bite of my own.

Maybe I was imagining it because I was still too turned on for my own good, but I was pretty sure his gaze slipped to watch as I slid the slice into my mouth, then took a bite.

"Let's just say, they both have their place," he agreed.

"A cheat day won't kill you."

"So, Fridays," he said. "You can order terrible food and force me to eat it."

He'd looked almost taken aback at his own words. Like he hadn't meant to say them. But I didn't want to let him take them back.

"I would love to watch your disgust at something truly atrocious. Like cheap, greasy tacos."

"Have some mercy," he demanded, eyes dancing as he finished off his first slice.

"None," I promised him.

And I meant it in more than one way.

The food, sure.

But also the shows for the cameras.

Now that I knew for sure he was watching.

And he was enjoying.

Oh, things were just getting started.

Seven

.

Fitz

Eventually, the damn contractor interrupted a lively debate about the best art movements, a subject she was decidedly more passionate about than I was, but one I had been educated on from a young age, so I could at least hold my own in the discussion.

I'd been enjoying it.

Admittedly, it had been a long time since I'd enjoyed the company of a woman. I'd been busy with work. We had a big merger coming up that had to go right. I hadn't even shared a meal with someone in the better part of six months, let alone anything other than that.

Which was what I was going to blame my creepy, horny jerk-off session on.

Frustration. Pent up from months of denying myself a couple of stolen hours with a woman to get a release.

That was all it was.

I mean, yes, sure, Wynn was objectively one of the most gorgeous women I'd ever seen, and, yeah, she had a shitton of wardrobe malfunctions for reasons completely beyond me, but it wasn't about *her* per se, just about what she represented.

Womanhood, sexuality, and availability.

That was it.

Nothing personal.

Though, speaking of personal, it was absolutely unacceptable for her to have been getting herself off in my house during work hours.

It would be grounds for dismissal, surely.

Except, as soon as that idea popped into my head, I mentally swiped it away. But only because she was the best damn house manager I'd had. That was the only reason.

I had just grabbed a coffee, and was heading back to my office to look over some things after the contractors and Wynn had finally gone home.

And it was there that something felt off.

The chair at the desk, I decided, looking at it. It was pushed all the way in. I'd been in too much of a panic to go get cleaned up to have pushed it in.

My heart started to pound in my chest as my gaze went to my laptop.

Wynn had been in the office when I'd come down to get the door for the pizza. Had she happened to see the footage on the laptop? The camera feed of the den where she thought she'd been having a private moment?

No.

No, if she knew that, there was no way she would have stuck around for dinner and conversation.

She would have run out of the house and never looked back.

Which only meant one thing.

She hadn't seen.

The screen had probably gone to a screensaver by the time she walked in.

Relief flooded through my system as I made my way to the desk. It wasn't until I was in my chair that I woke my laptop back up.

"What the..." I hissed as the screen flashed back up.

Not of the den like I'd been expecting.

No.

Of my master bathroom.

Where I'd gone after jerking off to clean up. You could still see my watch on the counter that I'd taken off before jumping in a cold shower.

I hadn't touched my laptop when I'd gotten up.

And the feed didn't skip between the cameras.

Which could only mean one thing.

Wynn had been watching *me* in a compromised situation.

No, not only that.

She'd known I'd been watching *her* in one, and then she'd watched me in one.

Yet she's said nothing. And she shared a meal with me. And she talked about seeing me after the weekend.

What kind of woman wanted to come back to a place full of cameras that could watch her every move?

"Huh," I said with a snort, as everything started to come together.

I guess it would be the same type of woman who had so many "innocent" wardrobe malfunctions every single day. I mean no one's tits popped out of their shirts as often as hers did. No one's skirts hiked up *just right* so that I could see her high, round ass that she never covered with anything other than a barely-there thong.

Wynn was an exhibitionist.

She liked to be watched.

It gave her some sort of thrill to know that the cameras were around, that she was putting on a show for them, that I might be watching her at any time, that she could get me hard without even looking at me, or being near me.

"Christ," I hissed, raking a hand down my face as I went into the cloud, and found the footage of her in the den.

I wasn't sure how the hell I'd missed it before. How she'd carefully positioned herself on the couch so I could watch as she fucked her pussy, as she teased her breasts.

She hadn't even been facing the TV she'd put on before sitting down. But the camera instead.

She was putting on a show.

For me.

Because she somehow knew I'd be watching.

Because she wanted me to watch.

"Fuck," I said, leaning back in the chair, feeling my cock stiffening again at those realizations.

I had to fire her. It was the only rational thing to do. I couldn't keep going on acting as if my employee wasn't whipping her tits out at work for me, that she wasn't flashing me her ass every chance she got, that she wasn't fingering herself because she knew I'd see, and wouldn't be able to control myself, would need to get some relief.

There was no way I could keep someone like that around.

It flipped the power dynamic, for one.

For two, it was a lawsuit waiting to happen if she ever became disgruntled for any reason.

And, for three, and maybe most importantly, I wasn't going to survive watching her in my house knowing I wasn't being a creep. That she wanted me to see.

I wasn't going to be able to do it.

Eight

Wynn

He hadn't called to fire me.

Honestly, I figured he would have sat down later, sometime before bed, reviewed the cameras, seen that I'd been on his laptop, and immediately called to tell me I'd overstepped a line, and canned me.

But the fact that he didn't could only mean one thing.

He knew that I knew about the cameras, and that I'd been using them to turn him on, and he wasn't upset by that fact.

Maybe I should have been off-put by that fact. I mean, most of the time, we were alone in that big, empty house. If he somehow saw my little performances as an invitation for more, he would be able to act on that. My objections would do me no good with no one around to step in if he chose to force himself on me.

I shouldn't have wanted to go back.

The game always ended for me once the voyeur knew I knew I was being watched. The fun had always been in the forbidden-ness of it all. But if the guy knew it wasn't actually forbidden, that, in fact, I was inviting it, it stopped having the same thrill. And, in the worst cases, it made the guys think I actually wanted them.

It was never about them.

I didn't get hot and bothered by the idea of their hands on me, but rather the way they couldn't control themselves because of me.

It was, at its core, a pretty narcissistic kink.

And it made no sense that I wanted to go back now that my boss knew what I was up to.

Maybe a part of me was intrigued by how this could excite me to know he knew, but have him say nothing, act on nothing, just quietly allow himself to be tormented day in and day out, knowing I was in his home, that I was within reach, but that he couldn't touch me.

That added a whole new layer of excitement I hadn't ever really anticipated.

I mean, if he ever tried something, I would be out of there.

But if he wanted to keep playing the game?

I was leaning toward playing as well.

At least for a while, see if it felt as good as it did in my mind.

Besides, the money.

I couldn't forget the money. I had a paid light bill and some new canvases just waiting for paint. Having that security was a big deal to me. I didn't want to screw it up all over a little fetish of mine. But so long as my job was secure, I figured it didn't hurt to keep screwing around a little bit. Especially now that I knew he was watching, and he knew I knew he was watching.

"Wynn, are you even listening?" Perry asked, dragging me out of my swirling thoughts, making guilt immediately overwhelm me. Because, well, no, I hadn't been listening.

In my defense, she'd been going on and on about her douchebag of a boyfriend, and there was only so many times I could say halfway nice, supportive things before I exploded and reminded her that she deserved so much better. Which would only upset her, then me, and cause a whole awful situation we'd been through too many times before.

"I'm sorry. No. I had my mind on work," I admitted, giving her a guilty smile.

"Oh, how is that going?" she asked, cupping her hot chocolate in her mitten-clad hands as we walked down the street, window shopping, occasionally telling each other to "remind me to pick that up for so-and-so for Christmas" even though we both knew we'd forget about whatever item it was before we made it up the next block.

"It's going great, actually. I wouldn't think a job with that much structure would be good for me. You know, like, creatively. But I've been doing a lot of pieces lately."

I was going to go ahead and leave off the fact that every one of those new pieces were borderline erotic in nature, all done through the lens of a voyeur fantasy. Images of women through keyholes or windows. Or that my most recent project was getting the world's most perfect male ass—which happened to belong to Fitzwilliam Buchanan—onto canvas. I'd stylized it a bit, putting the whole image in broad strokes of pinks, purples, yellows, and black, but there was no denying it was my boss's back and ass that was on display.

"Really? Oh, my God, Wynn. That's so great. I knew you were struggling there for a while because of bill stress."

I hadn't expressly told her that, but she'd put the pieces together since I'd always been talking about overdue bills and an issue painting since I'd gotten out of college.

"Yeah, I'm really happy about it," I admitted, even if a part of me was worried there might not be a market for the kind of art I was producing.

I would never know until I put them out there, right?

I mean, soup can paintings could be sold for like eleven million.

If Andy Warhol could make a mint on those, I could make a couple hundred off of my kinky, yet tasteful, canvases, right?

I was going to try, that was for sure.

"What about the cameras?" she asked, wincing at even the mention of them even as my body buzzed at the thought of them.

"The man is just security conscious. Besides, I only have to worry about them if I'm doing something I shouldn't be doing."

"They still freak me out."

"Maybe because you didn't really know Mr. Buchanan."

"And you do? He was rarely around."

"Well, I've been working late here and there, so I've come across him. He even asked me to share some pizza with him on Friday," I told her.

"What? No way. He always eat so healthfully."

"I think he only ordered it because I teased him about what he ate all the time."

"You teased Fitzwilliam Buchanan?" Perry gasped, pressing a hand to her heart. God bless her dramatic soul.

"I did."

"He doesn't seem like someone who would be okay with that sort of thing."

"Maybe you just think that because you've built him up in your mind to be some sort of royal or something," I suggested. "He's just a man."

With needs.

And urges.

And desires.

And it seemed like he might just desire me.

"That's probably true. It's hard not to think of him as, you know, more than the average person with his picture-perfect world."

"Picture perfect. Please," I scoffed. "Have you seen that atrocious art he has all around?" I asked, grimacing.

"Well, perfect aside from the art, of course," she played along, smiling. "I'm glad you're getting on with him. Maybe you were right. I was just being paranoid."

"You play that role beautifully, Per," I assured her, giving her hip a nudge.

"Have you taken a selfie in his amazing master bath yet?" she asked.

"No."

No, I hadn't.

But I was thinking maybe it was time.

—

The plan was simple.

I still wasn't ready to act like I knew he was watching.

I needed to be careful for my job's sake.

But there were all sorts of possible mishaps that could take place with regard to your wardrobe for positions like mine.

Like when I was cleaning it, *accidentally* turning the rainfall shower head on instead of the handheld attachment, soaking through my white shirt.

The shriek I let out was genuine even if the action itself hadn't been. Because, like I said, the water was frigid when it first came on.

"Shit shit shit," I hissed, jumping out of the shower, a little more drenched than I'd planned, and moved in perfect view of the camera, but was careful to avoid looking at it as I undid my sopping shirt.

I paused at the bottom button, anticipation sizzling across each nerve ending, enjoying the sensation for a moment before pulling the material open, exposing my breasts. My nipples were hard and straining from the cold water as I pulled off the shirt, holding it for a moment so the camera could get a good eyeful, before going to the sink to squeeze out the excess before hanging it up on the shower door.

I turned my back to the camera as I slipped out of my shoes then undid my pants, shimmying out of them, giving the camera a view of my mostly bare ass as I leaned forward to gather my wet pants, laying them across the top of the soaking tub.

Finished, I took a deep breath, turning, then making my way toward the bedroom, taking the show on the road, if you will.

See, there was a flaw in my plan, though.

The plan hinged on one thing.

My boss being at work watching the cameras, or at home after I left, reviewing the footage with a glass of his red wine.

Red wine that costs over a hundred dollars a bottle, I might add.

But, well, Fitzwilliam Buchanan was being a slacker.

Meaning he was home in the middle of the day.

Barreling into his room so fast that I didn't even have a chance to squeal before he was slamming into me.

"Shit," he hissed, hands grabbing my hips to prevent me from falling over.

Which was when he realized one vital piece of information. His hands met bare skin. Because I didn't have any clothes.

I watched as his handsome face went from frustrated to surprised to something darker, something sinfully dark as his gaze slid down to look at my almost nude body.

His hands fell immediately, some part of him holding onto the roles of our professional positions. But he couldn't seem to force his gaze away as he took long, greedy looks at my breasts, my stomach, the barely-there pink material between my thighs.

"Wynn..." he said, voice rough with desire.

When I glanced down, I could see the hard line of him against his slacks.

Remembering myself and my role, my hands slapped over my body, criss-crossing to cover as much of it as possible.

"Mr. Buchanan," I said, and I didn't have to fake the breathlessness to my voice. "I, ah, I wasn't expecting you. I was, um, cleaning your shower. And I had a mishap with the water. My clothes got sopping wet," I went on, watching as he took in what I said, and mixed it with what he was beginning to know about me, then coming to his own conclusions.

That it hadn't been a mishap.

That I'd been doing it on purpose.

"Maybe," he started, then had to clear his throat to speak past the husky edge his voice had taken on. "Maybe you should finish," he suggested.

"Finish what?" I asked, genuinely confused.

"Your task," he clarified. "Maybe you should finish cleaning the shower," he told me, eyes molten.

I felt a similar heat spread through my core as I realized what he was suggesting.

"Right. Yes, of course," I agreed, keeping my tone calm, even, like there was nothing at all unusual about the situation. "I will get to that," I added, taking a step away, giving him just long enough to look over my front as I dropped my arms, before turning and giving him a view of my ass as I walked away.

Did I put just a little bit more oomph in my step as I walked back into the bathroom? Absolutely I did.

As I climbed back into the glass shower stall, bending forward to grab the scrub brush I'd dropped, I noticed my boss moving around his massive bed, sinking down on the side, legs spread wide, elbows rested on his thighs, his hands steepled in front of that generous, delicious-looking mouth of his.

Watching.

God, yes, *watching*.

It turned out I was wrong.

The thrill wasn't gone because he knew that I knew he was watching. If anything, the knowledge muddled with the proximity of him was making the desire transition from a dull ache to an acute pain between my thighs as I grabbed the spray bottle, and started to clean once again.

But this time, I was all-too-aware of the way my body moved with each motion, the way my breasts swayed as I scrubbed the marble walls, the way my ass jutted out when I bent to retrieve the handheld attachment to rinse the cleaner down the wall.

I repeated the process with my back to him, feeling his heated gaze burning a hole through the glass, and blazing against my bare ass.

I stretched it out as long as I could, but there came a point where the shower couldn't get any cleaner, which had me turning to face him as I reached once more for the detached shower head.

But this time, I didn't spray down the walls.

Oh, no.

I rinsed my hands, then my arms, up over my shoulders, feeling the cool water harden my nipples once again, sending a shiver through my body.

I released the shower head, cutting off the water, and reaching for a bar of soap instead. Taking a step back, I leaned on the back wall of the shower, as I started to suds the bar up in my hands before running them up my arms, over my shoulders, then, finally, my breasts, letting out a small, barely audible whimper at the contact against skin that was aching so badly for touch.

I was sure he couldn't have heard it, but the acoustics of the shower must have been better than I realized because I watched as he dropped his hands from his face, reaching instead toward his belt and pants, working both free with quick, frustrated fingers.

Desire pinged off every nerve ending, thrummed through my chest and between my thighs as I watched him reach into his pants, pulling out his thick, straining cock with one of those big hands of his.

Fitz's greedy gaze slid to me, taking lingering moments over my breasts, my belly, then my thighs that I was rubbing together as though the brief pressure and friction was doing anything to ease the ache between. If anything, it was only making it worse.

It wasn't until his gaze moved up, those brilliant blue eyes that could make a woman's heartbeat skitter—or maybe that was just me—landed on my face that I could see just how desperate he was as well. Dare I even think, just as desperate as I was feeling in that moment.

Too far gone to care.

That was how I felt right then.

My brain was short-circuiting, unable to think clearly past the currents of desire that chased away any rational thought I should have had in that moment about the final lines that were about to be crossed, that I knew I couldn't jump back behind after.

But I didn't care.

I couldn't.

Not with the need pinging off every nerve ending, leaving me feeling frazzled and a little crazed from the overstimulation.

With an exhale that shook through my chest, my hand lowered over my belly, the bar of soap slipping from my grasp to thump and slide across the tile floor as my hand kept moving lower, lower, feeling the line of my panties, then slipping beneath.

It wasn't until my head fell back on a whimper as my fingers found my clit that Fitz's hand began to move, starting to stroke his hard cock.

My breath felt caught in my chest as my fingers kept moving over my clit, kept driving myself up under Fitz's intense gaze.

His breathing went fast and shallow, his strong chest heaving under his suit jacket and black shirt as his fist kept stroking himself, as his gaze stayed fixated on me.

My soft whimpers became throaty moans as I felt my walls tightening, as my body teetered on the edge before tossing me down into the depths of pleasure, leaving me crashing over and over as I forced my gaze to stay open, stay on Fitz as his body tightened, as his breath rushed out of him on a quiet groan, as he came along with me.

My eyes drifted closed for all of ten seconds, I swear.

But when they opened again, the spot on the bed where Fitz had been sitting was abandoned.

And just like that, the moment was over.

And reality was rushing back in, knocking my breath out of me as it pulled me under its merciless tidal wave.

"Shit. Shit shit shit," I hissed, ducking to grab the soap, putting it back in place, then the detached shower head before climbing out, drying off, and grabbing my clothes. A shiver coursed through me as the cold, wet fabric met my skin.

But it was good.

Bracing.

It kept me in the current moment.

You know, where my job was possibly on the line.

When I made my way back out of the bathroom, my boss was nowhere to be found.

By the time I got to the front window, he was already peeling out of the driveway, leaving me unsure and anxious about my future as his house manager.

Surely, he couldn't just go on as if nothing had happened.

But then the day came to an end, and I hadn't heard from him. So I went home, turning off my phone, and turning my swirling thoughts and knotted stomach into art, sure that when I finished and powered up my phone again, there would be a call or text telling me I was done.

It never came, though.

So, I showed up for work the next day.

And the day after.

Fitz just made sure never to be anywhere near me again.

It took over a week to have my nerves calm enough to let me think about the cameras again.

I'd been nervous at first, something new for me when it came to putting on a show for someone.

But, as the weeks stretched on, I got more and more daring.

Until, eventually, I found myself on his very bed with my skirt hiked up, and my fingers buried in my pussy, getting off where he slept to thoughts of him rolling me around those very sheets.

Still, nothing.

If we happened to be in the same house together at the same time, he stayed behind a locked door, avoiding, ignoring me, making me wonder if he was even looking anymore.

It was a thought that bothered me more than he should have, that he didn't want to watch me anymore.

It bothered me so much to make me desperate enough for the thrill that I took some extreme measures...

Nine

Fitz

My fucking bed smelled like her for two days until the bed was stripped and washed.

It was fucking embarrassing how disappointed I'd been to come home after a long day and find my bedding smelled like laundry detergent instead of Wynn's vanilla and rose scent, instead of the faint trace of her pussy from finger-fucking herself in the place where I slept, leading me to fevered dreams and a straining cock that no amount of self-gratification could satiate.

After her scent was gone, though, I had nothing left.

Because I could never cross that line we'd already crossed again.

The reasons were endless.

But the top contenders were that it was an abuse of power on my part, one that could get me sued if I wasn't careful to put an end to it, but it was also a bad idea solely because she was damn good at her job, and I didn't want to have to replace her.

I had to stop it before things got carried away.

I never would have known how strongly the urge would be to sneak around and find her in a compromising situation again, or simply to turn on the camera feed and wait for her skirt to hike up or her shirt to open.

I wouldn't have ever said I was into voyeurism.

But there was no denying I'd been into watching Wynn.

I damn sure had never been into exhibitionism before.

But I had stroked my cock while she'd watched.

I didn't know what the fuck was going on with me, if it was the merger, or the lack of sex, or what, but I needed to get a fucking grip.

Which was why I was working late at the office. To avoid running into her at home.

It was also why I was just barely resisting the urge to check my camera feed.

The goddamn things were put up for reasons that had nothing to do with my never-ending string of house managers. And that reason meant I was supposed to be checking them. But I didn't want to risk catching sight of Wynn's bare ass as she bent over to fetch something off the floor, or her tits bursting out of her top, filling my mind with ideas of taking her from behind, of wrapping that long, silky blonde hair of hers around my fist as I did so, of her pert breasts bouncing around as I fucked her harder and harder as she cried out, begging for release.

"Fuck," I hissed, feeling myself harden even with the passing thought.

It had been weeks.

Weeks.

And I still couldn't get her out of my mind.

"What's with the mood?" my brother asked, running his fingers over the spines of the books in my study. Why, I had no idea, since Blake had never willingly picked up a book. Hell, I was pretty sure he never unwillingly did so either. It was a well-known fact that he'd out-sourced all of his assignments in high school and college. And when that wasn't enough, that our father had paid off the teachers and professors to just keep moving along.

It wasn't that Blake was dumb. He was just a different kind of smart. Cunning and clever were words that came to mind. He had a lot of potential if he only tried to apply himself.

Maybe someday.

I couldn't expect him to bust his ass to prove himself like I had done my whole life. He didn't need to like I had. He was never going to take over the company after our father passed. That was always going to come to me. Which was why I'd worked so hard to prove myself worthy of that responsibility.

A part of me was hard on Blake because there was a little bit of envy on both our sides. Him, my wealth. Me, how carefree his life had been, the ability he had to really wild out and enjoy his youth. It was time I'd never get back, time I spent in boardrooms and flying back and forth across the country, trying to schmooze new clients, time I'd spent read-read-reading endless books on business and leadership. Time well spent? Objectively, likely yes. But also time I didn't get to spend enjoying my life.

And there was no denying that Blake enjoyed the fuck out of his life. There was hardly a weekend that didn't involve some sort of over-the-top party in the guest house where he lived, one that inevitably ended up spilling into the main house, no matter how many times I told him it was off-limits.

"Work," I told him. "You know, where you put in labor of some form in exchange for money in your bank account," I said, watching him shoot me a smirk because we both knew he hadn't exactly *earned* his paycheck in a couple of weeks.

He should have been fired, nepotism be damned.

But I'd promised my father on his deathbed that I'd take care of Blake, even when he didn't deserve it.

"Ah, yes, labor. It seems I'm allergic to it," he declared, dropping down in the chair in front of my desk, kicking up his feet on the edge simply because he knew it pissed me off.

Brothers.

It didn't seem to matter how old they got, certain aspects of that relationship would never seem to mature. Pushing buttons was a seminal favorite activity.

"That's the story now," I mumbled, closing the top of my laptop. "So to what do I owe the pleasure? I paid your liquor delivery bill last night, by the way."

"Gee, he must have come to your door by mistake," Blake said, lips twitching.

"Yeah, that must be it," I agreed, snorting.

"I wanted to tell you that some of the furniture in the pool room needs to be replaced. Must have been cheap shit," he added.

More like he allowed guests to stand on it.

"I'll check it out," I said, exhaling hard.

"You need to relax," Blake declared. "Maybe have that pretty house manager of yours get you an at-home massage. Maybe she'd give you one herself."

"No."

"Maybe I can get one from—"

"*No*," I snapped. I hadn't meant for it to come out as ferocious as it had. Blake even looked a bit taken aback. "I've gone through, what, five, house managers this year. This one is sticking. Don't fuck her," I ordered.

"Sounds like I'm not the one who needs to get fucked," Blake said, pulling his legs off my desk, standing, shooting me a raised brow look, then walking out.

He wasn't wrong.

That was the most annoying thing about my brother. He had this irritating trait of being right a lot of the time when it came to me.

I did need to get laid.

And I would.

As soon as the merger was final.

I would walk out of that boardroom, right into the closest bar, find a woman who was interested, and get out all these months of frustration with her.

Not Wynn.

It could never be Wynn.

With a sigh, I stood up from my desk, rolling my neck, and making my way through the house, ready to check out the damage to the pool room, so I could get new furniture ordered.

The room was at the back of the house, a giant room of windows from the walls to the ceiling. It was dominated by a large indoor pool with a dark liner. The floors were a brown so deep it was almost black, and the furniture was a mix of wooden tables and chairs and wicker conversation sets with dark cushions.

I liked to start most of my workdays with some laps in the pool before I showered. I found that exercise in the morning chased away the sleep tugging at my ever-tired eyes and brain. It gave me the energy I needed to get through my long days.

It would piss me off to go there every morning and see broken furniture all around.

It wasn't as bad as Blake had made it sound. Someone had clearly tried to stand on one of the wicker chairs, and had promptly fallen through it. One of the tables had been knocked over, and a hunk of wood had been chipped off it. But that was the extent of it.

On a relieved sigh, I dropped down on one of the wicker chairs in the corner near some giant ass plant that I was pretty damn sure hadn't been there the last time I'd swam laps on Friday morning.

But who would bring plants into the house?

Even as I thought that, though, the person in question came walking in with another massive, but different, plant, half-dragging it over to the other corner of the pool room, setting it up near the windowed wall closest to the sprawling backyard.

The view was something I took a few precious moments to soak in every morning. Chest heaving from the laps, I would fully surface, and move to the side of the pool, resting my arms on the tile, and watching as the sun started to get brighter and brighter, giving me a view of the seemingly endless grounds, made a little stark by winter, sure, but beautiful when it snowed, and would soon be green and colorful again as spring rolled in to chase the cold away.

I let my mind wander then, as well, for a few moments.

I pictured one day watching kids running around that yard, squealing, happy, looking a little bit like me, and a little bit like whoever their mom would end up being.

Someday, I would assure myself.

Someday after the merger, after life got back to normal, after I had some time to find the right woman, spend some time getting to know her, then committing my future to her.

My father had done so with my mom, though she'd died tragically young, leaving him a bitter workaholic who screwed around without strings, which, eventually, resulted in Blake.

I didn't want that.

I wanted the real thing, like what he had with my mother.

Someday.

I watched as Wynn twisted and turned the oversized pot until she got the plant how she wanted it, then took a step back, hands going to her hips, surveying the scene, giving me one stolen moment of privacy to get to look at her.

I'd been starved for so long.

I feasted on her.

She had on what I'd come to call her "usual uniform." Meaning a skin-tight pencil skirt, this time in plain black. Her top was an almost see-through white with black trim. It tucked into the skirt, but the buttons had been mostly left open in the front, letting me see a sliver of skin from her neck, between her breasts, and part of her belly before it cut off.

Her long blonde hair was pulled up into a careless clip, and I had an almost overwhelming urge to get up, walk over, remove the clip, and run my fingers through the soft-looking strands.

I curled my hands into fists and kept them on the arms of my chair as I watched her turn toward the windows, looking out onto the grounds, taking a slow, deep breath.

And then, almost as if she heard the silent wish, her arms lifted, carefully removing the clip, then shaking out her hair before smoothing it with one hand.

I watched as she kicked out of her black flats, flexing her soles against the cold tile, and rolling her neck.

Her hands disappeared then, and I had no idea what they were occupied with until I saw her shirt slipping out of her skirt.

Shit.

No.

Goddamn it, I worked so hard to avoid seeing her as she put on one of her exhibitionist displays.

And there I was, trapped. There was no way to escape without her seeing me leaving.

Maybe she was just going to flash the yard, hoping someone might be around to see. Then, disappointed, pull herself together, and get back to work.

And I could go take an ice-cold shower.

But the longer I watched, the less likely that reality seemed to be.

Wynn spread her shirt, sure, but she pulled it off entirely, giving me a peek of her sloped back. I'd never thought of a back as sexy before, but hers sure as fuck was.

When her hands disappeared again, I knew it was to remove her skirt. Sure enough, they hooked into her waistband and started to pull down.

Slowly.

So fucking slowly.

A genuine striptease for her invisible audience.

My cock was rock-hard by the time her skirt slipped under her ass, showing off the plump cheeks and the barely-there strip of her black thong.

Bending forward slowly, she slipped the skirt all the way down before straightening, and stepping out of it.

She stood there for a long moment, staring off into the yard. Innocently, even, just enjoying the view.

Then, she was moving, her gaze lowered as she turned.

Fuck.

And there she was, almost entirely bare again.

It didn't matter that I'd seen her just like this before. It was a kick to the gut, to the balls.

That gentle curve to her hips, the slope of her stomach, the swells of her breasts that I'd spent far too much time imagining covering with my palms, feeling those dusky pink nipples hardening against my hands before rolling them with my fingers, twisting, pulling, and wrapping my lips around them, feeling her arch up into my mouth as my tongue circled her.

My breath felt caught in my chest as she made her way toward the pool, her gaze on the depths within. Her leg extended, allowing her toe to tease across the surface of the water. Her breath caught and held for a second before releasing.

I kept the pool just a shade cooler than complete comfort, liking the bracing sensation first thing in the morning.

Wynn's hand slid up the sides of her thighs, then hooked the strip of her thong with her fingers, slowly lowering them down.

Like she was doing it just for me.

No.

Not for me.

She didn't know I was there.

She was just taking her clothes off so she could have a quick dip, but then be able to slip back into all dry clothing.

It had nothing at all to do with me.

Carefully, she stepped out of her thong, leaving the black fabric on the tile.

I tried to keep my gaze there instead of the newly bared part of her body. It was a valiant effort, but I maybe lasted all of fifteen seconds before my eyes drifted up her thighs, then the space between.

As though she felt my gaze fixated there, Wynn extended one leg forward, testing the water again, giving me a slightly better view. Then she was lowering herself down to her knees, slipping onto her ass, then twisting her legs forward, slipping them into the water.

She sat there for a long moment, kicking her legs in the water as her hands grabbed the sides of the pool. But then she was raising one arm up over her head. Then the other, grabbing the wrist of the first, and pulling, arching herself to the side. She repeated the stretch on the other side before sliding her hands back on the tile behind her, then leaning backward, arching her chest, putting her perfect tits on display.

She stayed that way for what felt like an eternity, yet not nearly long enough, before slowly slipping forward, going down into the water, and completely hiding her body from my prying eyes.

It was a long moment of watching nothing but her profile before she raised her arms outward and leaned back. Floating. Fucking floating on the top of the water.

Which made her breasts press out to be devoured by my ravenous gaze.

One of her legs kicked gingerly as her hair spread out across the water, a golden halo that looked even softer in the water.

One of her arms moved inward, softly stroking over her breast.

And it was right then that her head tilted and her gaze landed on me, a soft smile teasing her lips.

She knew.

She'd known from the moment she'd started to strip out of her clothes that I was there, that I was watching.

Fuck.

Her legs rose up, then pulled in, meeting her chest for the barest of seconds before she was twisting them to right herself upward again.

She stayed there for a long, daring second, gaze fixed on mine, before that smirk stretched wider, and then disappeared as she dove under the water and started to swim a lap.

Almost as if she was saying *Catch me if you can. If you dare.*

I was on my feet and kicking out of my shoes before I could even think the better of it.

I had enough common sense to drop my phone on the chair before I made my way to the pool stairs as she started her lap in that direction.

I could.

I dared.

And I was done denying myself the one thing I wanted.

Her.

Ten

Wynn

Of course I'd known he was in the pool room. That was the main reason I'd gone in there.

I mean, sure, I had just hauled all the plants out of the garage that I'd gotten dropped off from the local nursery. But there were ones I'd wanted to move into other parts of the house as well. I didn't *have* to put the ones in the pool room first.

But when I'd seen him heading off in that direction, likely to see the damage Blake's party guests had done, so he could replace the furniture—a task I had already done the legwork of, and was just waiting to show him the order to sign off on—I saw it as one last chance to entice the man.

I told myself this would be it.

I wouldn't do it again.

I would just get my one last fill, and then I would find a way to keep my presence in his home strictly professional. I could find some new target outside of work to fulfill my fantasies with.

With that decision in mind, I'd taken my time with it. No flirty bend-overs to show off my ass, or sudden movements that made my boobs pop out.

Oh, no.

I did a full-on striptease beside that pool, making every single movement slow and sensual, wanting to drive him to the brink before I was even fully naked, and then push him over as I leaned back beside the pool, as I got in and floated, knowing full well that my breasts would glide just above the surface of the water, that the dark liner would obscure most of what else was beneath. A peekaboo effect that would drive any man out of his mind with need.

One look at his face said I'd accomplished my goal.

His eyes were blue fire, sparking, igniting, burning across every inch of exposed skin.

That was the thrill I needed.

Him liking what he saw.

Him wanting me.

Telling myself that would be enough, that I needed to at least attempt to make it look like I wasn't trying to drive my boss crazy, I dunked under the water, then started to swim some laps.

To make it look like swimming had always been my intention, sure. But also to burn off some of the excess sexual energy that was pinging off every nerve ending, making me feel frazzled and fuzzy, a little more out of control than usual.

I needed the exercise to get my mind right again.

That was all I was expecting.

So I threw everything into it.

I hadn't been expecting, well, him.

To have had enough.

To lose the grip on his control.

All I knew was that one moment, I was swimming laps.

The next, hands were reaching into the water, grabbing me at my sides, and lifting me upward.

I barely had a chance for my eyes to open, to take in my boss standing in the water fully dressed, before his lips were crashing down on mine.

Harder, hungrier than I even could have imagined.

Fitzwilliam Buchanan had always come across as cool, calm, collected, and completely in control over himself.

He had no control right then, though, as he turned me, slamming me back against the unyielding wall of the pool as his lips slanted over mine.

Fitz's hand rose, grabbing the back of my neck with borderline painful pressure as his lips bruised into mine for a long moment.

I was helpless to do anything but kiss back.

I didn't *want* to do anything but kiss him back.

It should have ruined it.

That was what I always thought in my head. If things went from exhibition and voyeurism to actual physical touch, the magic would be gone for me, I would be over it.

But I was far from over it.

The magic was alive and well.

It sizzled across my nerve endings, the heat mixed with the cold water creating a strange sort of chaos in my overstimulated system, making me tremble hard once. Enough that Fitz felt it, his lips suddenly going more gentle, more explorative. His hand softened on my neck, massaging absentmindedly as his mouth got to know mine.

This close, I could smell the spicy scent of his cologne I'd caught myself sniffing more than a few times. Once, I'd even put a tiny spritz on my bare breasts before buttoning up my shirt again, having the strange urge to smell him on me as I went about my day. It mingled with the tangy, sharp aroma of the chlorine in the pool, making me feel a little fuzzy, a bit drunk on it all.

And that was before his hand left my neck and started to roam.

Fitz's teeth snagged my lower lip hard enough to make me gasp. Taking the opportunity, his tongue slipped inside, claiming mine as his palm glided down my back, moving over the flare of my hip, slipping around to my belly, then sliding up.

My stomach tightened as his fingertips traced the underside of one breast, then the other, making my cold-hardened nipples twist even tighter as the desire bloomed across my core, spreading outward until it went from a dull ache to a painful need between my thighs.

My back arched, pressing my chest outward, silently begging for his touch as my hands slid up his arms, over his shoulders, remembering the outlines of his muscles as I did so, thinking about feeling his bare skin.

Mind on the task, my hands slid downward, grabbing the first button of his shirt and working it free with surprisingly clumsy fingers. Then the second, the third, the fourth. It was there I had to pause, grabbing his shirt in my hands and yanking it out of his pants before continuing.

Finished, I took a breath so deep it shook my chest as my hands flattened on Fitz's stomach, just resting there for a moment, feeling the way his muscles tensed under my touch before slowly moving upward, tracing the indents of his abdominal muscles, feeling the strength in his chest.

His lips pulled from mine, and my eyelids drifted open, looking up at him, already finding his intense gaze on me, eyes pools of desire that made another rush of need move through me as I pushed the shirt off of his shoulders, dropping it onto the water behind him.

My hands moved downward again, over his back, then around to his hips before tracing up his chest, then encircling his neck.

Taking a deep breath, I pressed inward, closing the distance between our bodies, feeling my breasts crush to his chest.

A low sigh escaped me as a rumbling sound moved through Fitz, vibrating into my chest.

His hands moved from my hips to sink into my ass, squeezing hard, pulling my body even closer as his lips slanted over mine again.

Hard, hungry again.

One of his hands shifted down slightly, grabbing the back of my thigh, angling it up, and coaxing it around his back, spreading me open for him. And as soon as I was, his pelvis pressed forward, pinning me back against the wall of the pool again, but this time with his hard cock straining against his pants, and pressing against my pussy.

His mouth muffled the sound of the moan that escaped me as my hips did a small circle, getting a hint of the friction I needed.

More.

I needed more.

I lifted my other leg, made almost weightless by the water, and wrapped it around Fitz's lower back, then used that leverage to writhe against his hardness, driving myself upward, closer to that edge, nearer to release.

Fitz's lips ripped from mine, trailing down the side of my neck instead as he pushed me back against the wall, and started grinding himself against me.

Slow at first, then gaining in speed, in intensity, in pressure.

Before, suddenly, he yanked away, breaking the contact.

A slow, sexy smile toyed at his lips at the sound of my objection. It was the sort of self-satisfied smirk that would be irritating if it wasn't so well deserved.

"Fitz," I whimpered, trying to move closer.

At the sound of his name on my lips, a low, feral, growling noise moved through his chest as one of his hands grabbed my hip, sinking in so hard that I was sure there would be bruises left in their way. It was a fact that shouldn't have made me feel all tingly, yet somehow managed to anyway.

His other hand slipped under the surface of the water, and for a long moment, I didn't know his intention. Not until his finger slipped between my thighs, traced up my cleft, then started to circle my clit.

The moment, I was sure, couldn't have possibly gotten any hotter. That was until Fitz moved his thumb to my clit, then slipped two fingers inside of me, his exhale shaking through his chest as my walls tightened around his fingers.

My impatient hips rocked against his palm, and I watched as Fitz cracked his neck to the side in a show of frustration. And, God, did I love seeing him starting to lose his control.

Before I could get too drunk off of watching him, though, he was suddenly lowering down in front of me, running a line of kisses over my one clavicle, then the other, before moving between, resting his forehead against the space between my breasts for a long moment, taking slow, measured breaths as his fingers started to fuck me.

Slow.

So incredibly, frustratingly slow.

At the sound of my first moan, his breath released, exhaling warm air over my cold breasts, making a shiver course through me a second before his head shifted, and his lips closed over one of the hardened peaks of my nipples.

I very nearly came right then and there.

But some sick, masochistic part of me wanted more of this sweet torture.

My back arched, pressing my breast further out as his tongue traced, as his teeth nipped, as his lips sucked.

"Fitz, please," I begged, my hips rocking against him, needing more.

His lips released one nipple only to go across my chest to continue the torment.

But this time, his fingers started to move faster, thrusting in and out of me as his thumb worked my clit.

From over his shoulder, a movement caught my eye. The door to the sprawling guest house that was practically its own estate, opened.

And out walked Blake.

I should have said something. I knew it was the right thing to do. But I leaned forward instead, pressing my lips into Fitz's neck as my hands roamed over his back, and my gaze watched Blake make his progress toward the back of the main house.

He could look over at any moment.

He could catch his brother finger-fucking my pussy.

He could stop to watch.

"So fucking tight," Fitz hissed as my walls tightened around him.

"Faster," I begged, noticing Blake getting closer before looking at Fitz again, finding his gaze hungry.

But I didn't know just how hungry.

Until his fingers left me, both hands sinking into my hips.

"I need to taste you," he told me, making my stomach flip-flop at his words before he was lifting me out of the water, and placing my bare ass on the tile.

His hands left my hips, sliding down the outsides of my thighs, then grabbing my knees, and spreading them wide.

Fitz's gaze went to mine for a moment before it slipped downward, gazing at my pussy for a long second before burying his face between my thighs.

I was aware of too many things at once. The brush of his soft hair on my inner thighs, the feel of his tongue as it traced my clit, the low groaning sound that escaped him as he tasted me, and the fact that Blake was closing in on the door to the kitchen. Just one short hallway away.

"Oh, my God," I whimpered, my hands grabbing the back of his head as my hips writhed against him.

I pulled up my legs, sliding them over his bare shoulders as I leaned backward until my back hit the tile.

My eyelids unexpectedly slid closed.

Experience told me I should have been looking to see if we were being watched.

But I didn't want to. I wanted to lose myself in the moment. I wanted to feel the way Fitz's tongue worked me with practiced precision, the way his fingers slid inside me again, but this time turned and stroked over my top wall, engaging my G-spot as he drove me *up up up*.

"*Yes*," I cried as his tongue started to move faster.

Vaguely, I heard the door in the kitchen open and close.

Blake could be on his way right that moment.

Fitz's body tensed, but my hands grabbed his head harder, holding him against me.

"Don't stop," I pleaded, trailing off on a moan as he got me right to that edge. "Please, Fitz," I cried, feeling myself teetering on that precipice for one agonizing moment.

Then his tongue circled.

His fingers stroked.

And I shattered.

I couldn't tell you if my breath got caught and I choked down my moan, or if I cried out in the big, empty room. All I could tell you is that the waves crashed over and over and over. And Fitz kept working me through them, dragging them out.

I came back down after, body trembling. Was it the cold from being out of the water or aftershocks from the orgasm? I had no idea. All I knew was my body was racked with them, making me feel uncommonly out of control.

"Fitz, that you?" Blake called, voice getting closer.

Fitz's head shot up, eyes wide, a little panicked.

I didn't have time to school my face into lines of false innocence. He saw the truth all over my face.

"You knew," he hissed even as he hauled himself out of the pool, water cascading down his soaked pants as he made his way toward the door.

Just in time.

Blocking Blake from coming in.

"What happened to you?" I could hear Blake ask.

"I tripped over broken furniture and fell in the pool," Fitz lied. I hate to say it, but the man did it so quickly, so smoothly, that it was somehow a turn on.

"Where's your shirt?" Blake asked, sensing something was up.

"What are you doing here?" Fitz shot back.

"I was looking for Wynn," Blake declared, piquing my curiosity.

I mean, yes, of course, I'd come across Blake several times since I started working for Fitz. He would pop in occasionally to steal some supplies since he had no house manager of his own and wasn't life-savvy enough to remember to pick up TP before he ran out, or laundry detergent until he went to do a load of wash and realized had none.

We talked, sure.

But we never engaged so often that he would seek me out.

"Why?" Fitz asked, voice getting a little rougher.

Like maybe he didn't like the idea of his little brother wanting to talk to me.

Jealousy had never been a turn on for me before, but there was no denying the warm sensation moving across my chest at his tone.

"I wanted to ask her something. Have you seen her around?"

"I don't know, Blake. I don't have tracking devices on my employees."

"Alright. I'll go find her," Blake said, and I could practically hear his shrug before he left.

Fitz stood there for a long moment, taking a deep breath, before turning toward me again.

I guess he was expecting for me to have taken the time to get up, to find my clothes, to get back into them.

But I was exactly where he left me. My arm was rested under my neck. The other was resting lightly on my lower stomach. And my gaze was on him.

"This can't happen again," he declared, voice tight, like it was hard to get those words out.

From the way his gaze hungrily moved over my body, I figured he didn't mean a single word of what he said.

"Okay," I agreed, voice sweet.

"I mean it," he insisted, making no move toward me. Instead, he went toward the far side of the pool, gathering my strewn clothes, then a towel before making his way in my direction.

My gaze followed him, but I didn't move otherwise.

As he moved in at my side, his head tipped back as he sucked in a deep, steadying breath before his eyes opened again.

"Okay," I said again, a soft smile teasing at my lips.

"Wynn..."

"Hmm?" I asked, making sure I took a slow, deep breath, making my breasts press out. He didn't miss the movement.

"You need to get dressed," he said, putting my clothes down on the closest chaise.

"Sure," I agreed, drawing my knees up into my chest, then shifting onto my side, going up on them right at his feet. Then angling my head up to find him looking down at me with fresh hunger in his eyes, likely thinking about me opening his pants, then my mouth, and slipping his hard length inside, sucking him with the same sort of passionate determination as he'd gone down on me with.

"Wynn." My name sounded like a curse on his lips as the hand that wasn't holding the towel balled into a tight fist, like he had to physically restrain himself from reaching out and touching me.

The surge of power inside me was heady, was something I wanted more of.

My hands reached out, grabbing his calves, then sliding upward. Over his thighs. Then to his hips. All the while, my gaze stayed on his, watching the mix of confusion and interest and heat as my hands teased the skin of his abs as they slid up the sides of his stomach, then, finally, outward, grabbing both of his arms, and pulling myself to my feet.

Slowly.

So freaking slowly.

I could practically feel his body shaking with repressed need as I carefully made sure my body brushed his. Just lightly enough that you could call it an accident, but hard enough that he felt the tips of my nipples and the swells of my breasts on his thighs, his stomach, then his chest as I stood before him.

Standing, my gaze held his for one long moment. Then another. Just long enough for me to soak in the way he needed me.

After getting my fill of that, I released his hands, turning slowly, giving him a view of my back.

"Towel?" I asked, voice soft.

"Right," Fitz said, clearing his throat, but even that didn't chase away the lingering tightness that came with desire in his voice.

He moved back a step to spread out the oversized towel as I raised my arms up over my head, pulling up my hair, giving him silent instructions to wrap it around me himself.

After a long pause, that was exactly what he did.

I wasn't faking the shiver that moved through me when his fingertips brushed the swells of my breasts as he carefully tucked the edge of the towel in. Did I go ahead and take an unnecessarily deep breath right then? Yes, yes I did.

And I wasn't imagining the almost pained noise that moved through Fitz's chest as I did.

"You need to get dressed, Wynn," he said, voice shivering over my skin.

"Yes, sir," I agreed, hearing that pained sound again a moment before he backed away from me.

He moved around my body, sopping wet.

"This won't happen again," he said, gaze not meeting mine.

"Okay, Mr. Buchanan," I agreed, noticing the flash of desire before he ducked his head, and moved away from me.

I watched his back as he walked off and disappeared into the house before I grabbed my clothes, and ducked into the bathroom off of the pool room, dressing, then towel-drying my hair before pinning it back up, then making my way out of the pool room, and into the kitchen.

Which was where Blake found me five minutes later, looking taken aback.

"What's up, Blake?" I asked, pretending to jot something down in my ever-present notepad.

"I was just in here looking for you," he said, and it almost came off like an accusation.

"Hm? Oh, yeah, I was restocking the paper products in the garage," I lied. Well, partially. I had done that before I'd gone into the pool room to chase Fitz, to get one more chance at putting a show on for him.

"Oh," Blake said, looking deflated by that news.

"Did you need something? To steal some more fabric softener, perhaps?" I asked. "I've never met anyone who has gone through that stuff as quickly as you do," I added.

"What can I say, I like my clothes soft."

"And with fabric softener marks," I said, reaching out to grab the sleeve of his shirt, showing him the slightly white spot.

"Whoops. Anyway, I had a request for the party."

"What party?" I asked, brows furrowing.

"The one my brother clearly forgot to tell you to plan," he said.

"What?" I hissed, heartbeat picking up as my mind started to race. "What party? When?"

"A work party for the clients he has been schmoozing for half a year and their wives. In a week and a half."

"Oh my God," I hissed, stomach sinking. "How could he forget to tell me that?" I asked, but was immediately answered by the memory of him avoiding me like the carrier of a viral plague. "Are you sure he isn't planning it himself?"

"I don't think he would know where to start for something like that."

He wasn't wrong.

"I, ah, I will have to ask him. What was your request?" I asked, flipping to a new page in my notebook and jotting down things that I would want done before he had company.

Like having the floors waxed and the carpets shampooed. Washing the drapes. Getting someone in to clean the windows and the ceiling fans and chandeliers that were too high for a normal ladder to reach.

"That you make sure he uses some other catering company. The food was complete shit last time."

"Okay. Noted. I will look up options, and bring them to him," I said, jotting that down. "Thanks, Blake," I added absentmindedly.

"Did you just take a shower?" he asked, halfway out of the door.

"What?" I asked, then remembered my hair. "Oh, no," I said, reaching up to touch it. "I didn't have time to dry it before work. I have thick hair," I added. "Takes forever to dry."

"Hm," Blake said in a way that made me think that if he hadn't outright seen his brother and me, he had suspicions.

Taking a deep breath, I straightened my clothes, grabbed my notebook, and charged through the house to confront Fitz about this supposed party.

Eleven

Fitz

It wasn't that I'd forgotten about the party, per se.

It was too important to have completely slipped my mind.

I guess the problem was I'd underestimated just how much work needed to take place to get my house—which always seemed reasonably ready for company—prepared.

Wynn had been unexpectedly prepared to tell me all the shit that needed to be done.

After sitting back a little slack-jawed at her list, she'd explained that her step-father was a businessman who often needed to host events, so she'd learned from a young age how to get a house ready for an event.

When I'd asked why she'd been the one to help rather than her mother, she'd given me a sort of sweet smile and declared that her mother was more the type of woman to spend her day out picking wildflowers for the tables than calling the cleaners or caterers.

And, in a way, I guess that gave me quite a bit of insight into Wynn.

She had a free-spirited mother that had likely instilled in her a love of art, thus encouraging her to go to school for it, but a business-minded, practical step-father that gave her the skills to self-start and be good at a more regimented job.

Not that I needed to be thinking any more about the woman than I already did.

Ever since the pool, all I'd done was think about the feel of her curves, the soft sighs that escaped her when I touched her, the taste of her pussy on my tongue.

It was enough to make me hard just thinking about it in passing while at work, while on my way home, while listening to the woman herself kindly but firmly boss people around my house over the next several days.

It was no use trying to avoid her, either. She was everywhere, seemingly handling ten different things at once. Even when I tried to shut myself into my office to keep away from her, not trusting myself fully not to reach for her again, to finish what we started in the pool.

Because it seemed like every twenty minutes or so, she had some reason to need to burst in to give me options, or for me to sign off on things.

The caterer, the menu, the drinks, the music.

And, invariably, she needed to discuss this with me while leaning over my shoulder. Her hair would always be tucked to one side, giving me the perfect view of her unconfined breasts that played peek-a-boo with her button-down shirt. And then there was her smell—rose and vanilla—that was impossible to ignore up close.

"Yeah?" I called to the familiar tap to my office door.

Wynn again.

Three soft fingertip taps.

That was her signature.

"Mr. Buchanan," she said. No, not said. She purred it. Or I just thought that because everything about the woman seemed to scream sexuality to me, intentional or not.

"Yes, Wynn?" I asked as I took a slow, steadying breath.

She looked unexpectedly worn-out.

She'd always been a hard worker, but she'd clearly been burning the candle at both ends if her eyelids looked so heavy, if there were slight bags under them.

She was wearing a simple dark green wrap dress instead of her usual button down shirt and pencil skirt. It was no less perfectly tailored to fit her, though, hugging every curve I now knew so well.

As she approached, quiet in her flat shoes, I could see the peaks of her nipples against the thin material of her dress, making my cock stir to life yet again.

That was all it took with her.

Her presence.

I didn't know what the fuck was wrong with me.

"Alright," she said, sighing heavily as she rounded my desk, dropping that perfect ass of hers onto the top of my desk right beside me, her leg actually touching my chair.

It was then that she raised that ever-present notebook of hers, flipping to a page, and giving her notes a nod.

"I think we have covered most of it," she declared. "We will have to greet the florists and the liquor store employees the morning of the party, obviously. And I will handle the caterers and the band before I head out."

"You're staying." The words were out before I even got a chance to really think about them. But there was no taking them back. What's more, I didn't *want* to take them back.

"I mean, everything should run smoothly. But if you want me to hang back in the kitchen or what have you, I can do that."

"Do you have a dress?" I asked, my tongue just doing whatever the fuck it wanted without input from my head.

"I wouldn't need a dress to be in the kitchen," she said, brows furrowing a bit.

"You won't be in the kitchen. Not all night," I added.

"Al...right," she said, looking no less confused. "I will get a dress," she agreed. "There is one last thing..." she said, trailing off, tapping her pen on her notepad.

"What's that?"

"Blake," she said, giving me a knowing look. "He's... he's had a lot of input about the party. I just want to make sure you're aware of that."

I wasn't.

And I wasn't happy to hear that either.

"I will have a talk with him to make sure he knows it isn't a free-for-all party." He should have known that, but you could never tell with Blake either.

"Okay, well, then that seems to be everything," she said, putting her notebook down beside my laptop.

I couldn't help but watch as she rolled her neck for a second before reaching up and behind her head to undo her hair clip. It was a motion that made her breasts strain against the thin material of her dress. And when she leaned back a bit further to work a kink out of her back, the goddamn wrap part slipped ever so slightly, giving me an eyeful of the swell of her breast.

I'd seen the woman fully naked. I shouldn't have been hard as a rock over a hint of breast. But there was no denying it, either.

I had no idea what kind of hold this woman had on me, but she'd become all I could think about when I was awake, all I dreamed about when I slept.

It needed to stop.

A little, niggling voice in the back of my head, though, was telling me that it was never going to stop. At least not until we could finish what we'd started in the pool.

Except, of course, we couldn't do that.

"You seem... tense," Wynn said, drawing my attention back upward where I found her with her arms resting behind her, making her back arch.

"N...no," I said, clearing my throat after hearing the roughness in my voice.

"Oh, hm. I must be mistaken," she said, doing a little shrug before slowly—so painfully fucking slowly—uncrossed her long legs in a movement designed to make her skirt hike up. Enough. Just enough to see she hadn't worn any panties to work. The realization made the desire like a vice grip on my balls. "Is something wrong?" she asked, feigning innocence even as she planted her damn foot on the arm of my chair, spreading herself wide for me.

"Wynn," I growled, forcing my gaze back upward. Where I found her balancing back on one hand as she dipped her damn pen in and out of her pouty lips.

"Yes?" she asked, all sweet, even if the light in her eyes told me she knew exactly what she had me thinking about.

"Stop," I demanded.

"Stop what, Mr. Buchanan?" she asked, damn near purring out my name. And I was forced to watch as that tongue of hers darted out, toyed around the curved top of the pen cap.

"You know what," I said, my voice a rumble as I forced my hands into fists on my thighs, trying to resist the urge to slip my fingers up her skirt, to slide them inside her pussy.

"I don't. You should tell me," she suggested as she started to glide the pen in and out of her mouth, filling my head with thoughts of those lips circling around my cock, working it up and down like she was doing to the damned pen. "Are you sure you're not tense?" she asked, a wicked smirk toying at her lips. "You seem a little... hard," she said as her foot *accidentally* slipped off the arm of my chair, her foot teasing over the head of my cock, making me see white for a second. "I mean... tense," she corrected even as she planted her foot on my upper thigh.

"I told you it can't happen again," I said even as she teased her toes over, circling around my straining cock.

"This?" she asked, curling her toes around the base of my cock and doing a small stroke. "I'm pretty sure we've never done this before," she told me, bringing in her other foot to wrap around the other side of my cock, then starting to jerk me off through my pants.

"Technicality," I hissed, leaning back in my chair, trying not to enjoy the sensations as much as I was right then, but finding it impossible to think past the growing sensations.

"Maybe," she agreed, feet moving away to plant on the floor beside my chair. "I think this might be a technicality too," she mused as she slid off the desk and onto her knees at my feet, her hands planted at my thighs and moving upward. "Right?" she asked as her fingers went for my button and zipper.

"Wynn..." I growled even as her hands reached inside to grab my throbbing cock, pulling it out of my pants, and grabbing it with both hands.

"Hmm?" she asked as her head ducked, as she ran her lips down and up my shaft on one side before doing the same to the other side, avoiding the head. Only when she was done with that did her gaze slip upward, holding mine. "What do you think, Mr. Buchanan, should I stop because of a technicality?" she asked as her tongue moved outward fully, openly inviting me into her mouth.

"No," I hissed, grabbed the back of her neck, and shoving her face down, feeling my cock slide into her welcoming mouth, pressing hard against the back of her throat as she let out a little gagging sound that only managed to make me harder still.

My hand eased on the back of the neck, wanting her to take over, so I could get lost in the sensations as she started to move, slow and torturous at first, then going faster and faster as my breathing started to hitch, as she dragged ragged groans out of me.

"Shit," I hissed, jolting upright, mind half-foggy from the need for release. But that was a car door I'd heard. "Wynn, door," I told her, reaching down to pull her back off me by her hair.

She released me.

But only to shoot me a wicked smirk with her eye makeup running down her face as she scooted backward, going under my desk, and grabbing my chair, pulling it forward.

"What? No," I insisted, even as a surprising thrill of desire coursed through me.

That was not the kind of man I was, the kind who got sucked off under his desk.

Or, perhaps, it was more accurate to say that never used to be the kind of man I was. Because, clearly, it was who I was now as I scooted a little closer to the desk, and grabbed the remote to turn the speakers on low just as the front door opened.

And in walked Blake as Wynn's tongue traced down the underside of my cock, then started to tease over the sensitive skin of my balls.

"Hey, do you know where Wynn is?" Blake asked, coming a couple feet into my study.

Oh, I knew where Wynn was, alright.

In fact, the second she knew we weren't truly alone anymore, her lips gently closed around one of my balls, sucking gently, damn near making me come right then and there.

"Why?" I asked, trying to focus on my breathing.

"I wanted to talk to her."

"About what?" I asked.

"The party. Her car is still outside. You haven't seen her?"

"It's a big house." *With lots of surfaces to climb under.* "What about the party did you need to discuss?" I asked, needing to curl my hand into a fist, nails biting into my palm, as Wynn's tongue moved back upward, and was circling around the head of my cock, lapping up the precum that had beaded up there.

"My list."

"This is a work event. You're not inviting your friends."

"Guests," Blake corrected.

"You get a date, Blake. A date, that's it. And if she could wear something that covers at least a third of her body this time, that would be appreciated."

"Fucking prude," Blake muttered as he walked off through the back of the house.

Prude.

While I had my house manager sucking me off under the desk.

Wynn's lips closed around me again, a low moan escaping her as she did so, the vibration moving through me, making my hips jerk upward, going deeper into her waiting mouth.

I could hear Blake banging around in the kitchen cabinets, but I was too far gone to care about him still being in the house.

Scooting the chair backward so I could see, I grabbed a handful of her hair, moving it out of the way. Then I watched as she mouth-fucked me like there was nothing else in the world she would rather do.

Fast, deep, messy, making me curl forward as the need for release grew. Her hand moved out, massaging my balls as she took me deeper, the head tapping the back of her throat with each downward motion.

My breathing got fast and ragged.

My entire body tensed.

"Fuck," I hissed, my hips rocking into her mouth as I got to that edge. "Just like that," I ground out as she started to twist her head around as she moved up and down my cock. "I'm going to come," I told her as my hand crushed into the back of her neck, making her take me deep, coming down her throat so hard that the world went black for a moment. And afterward, I was panting and boneless, folded forward in my chair, one arm braced on the desk as I tried to pull myself together.

Wynn let my cock slide out of her mouth, then took the time to tuck me back away before sliding backward, rising up, and sitting off the edge of the desk again, making it so I had to lean back to look up at her.

Mascara ribbons stained her cheeks, her lips were swollen, and her skin flushed. But that look in her eyes? Pure fucking triumph.

It was the sexiest thing I'd ever seen in my life.

And it lasted all of five seconds before I could hear Blake calling out as he moved closer, "Did you say something to me?"

"Shit," I hissed as Wynn moved away from the desk, eyes huge, knowing what her face looked like.

Then, I shit you not, this woman slammed her foot against my desk at almost full force, then fell down onto the spare chair.

"Ow ow ow ow ow," she hissed, cradling her foot in her hands just as Blake came into the room, taking in the scene with a furrowed brow.

"You okay, Wynn?" he asked as I started to genuinely wonder if she'd really hurt herself.

"She slammed her foot into my desk," I told my brother as he moved in closer.

"Are you crying?" he asked as Wynn lifted her head. And, sure enough, there was a glisten of tears in her eyes that could explain the black streaks on her face. "Did you break something?" he asked, dropping down, reaching out toward her.

"Don't touch her," I snapped, my voice a whip cracking in the quiet room, making the both of them stiffen and look over at me. To be honest, I was surprised at the ferocity in my tone, in the tug of possessiveness in my chest. "She didn't say you could touch her," I added in a much more even tone. "Do you want a sexual harassment complaint?" I asked.

"Glad to see you care so much about the people who work for you," Blake said, voice tight.

"I'm fine," Wynn insisted, seeming to sense the growing tension between us. "Really. I'm just a big baby about this kind of thing," she added, flexing her toes a couple times. "Your brother told me that you will be bringing a date," she added, accepting the handkerchief I handed across the desk to her to wipe at her cheeks.

"I, ah, yeah."

"What's her name?" she asked.

At that, Blake shot her a boyish smile. "I don't know yet," he admitted.

"Typical," Wynn said, shaking her head as she got to her feet. "Well, be sure to tell her that the event is formal. If she doesn't know what that means, you can give me her number, and I can send her some examples," she told him. It was such a slick way of putting him in his place that I wasn't even sure he caught on.

"Okay. Sure. Sounds good. Where are your shoes?" he asked, making me stiffen.

"Oh. The must have gone flying when I tripped."

"I thought you hit your foot."

"Well, both. I tripped over my own feet, and lost my shoe, then slammed my foot into the desk as I tried to right myself. I don't know where the other shoe got to," she added, starting to look around, which made Blake do the same as I quickly kicked them away from my side of the desk.

"Over there," I said, drawing their attention behind Blake.

"Don't strain yourself to get up and get it," Blake mumbled, retrieving the shoe as Wynn did her best to hold in a smile.

"Thank you, Blake," she said, slipping her feet back into her shoes. "I should get going," she said.

"Yeah, me too," Blake agreed, nodding, making his way to the doorway. "Goodnight, Wynn."

"'Night, Blake," she called before turning back to me as she leaned in the doorway to the foyer.

Taking a deep breath, I got to my feet, moving across the study, and slowing as I passed her.

"We're done. That's it. Never again."

"Mmhmm," she said, a soft smile playing at her lips.

"I mean it," I added more firmly.

"Of course you do," she agreed, talking to my back as I walked into the foyer, then toward the stairs because, quite frankly, I didn't trust myself not to turn right around, grab her, and give us what we both knew we wanted.

"Wynn..."

"Goodnight, Mr. Buchanan," she called in a sing-song voice, one that said she knew damn well she had the upper hand, and wasn't above using it again when the mood suited. "Have pleasant... dreams," she added as she made her way toward the front door. "I will see you for the party," she finished, shooting me a smile when I turned to watch her back out of the door.

I'm not proud to admit that I watched through the window from my position on the steps as she made her way down the front path and slid into her car. I watched, too, as she bounced around in the front seat of her beat-up car, trying to keep herself from freezing as the heat warmed up.

I should get her a car.

What?

What the fuck was that?

I didn't buy random women cars just because their cars were old and unreliable.

But I could buy her a car if her old and unreliable car meant she might not be able to perform her job.

Jesus Christ.

What the hell was wrong with me?

Back in her car, the heat must have gotten warm enough for Wynn to crank up the air, judging by the way her hair was dancing around her shoulders as she strapped in, then pulled out of the driveway.

Fuck.

I needed to get it together.

At least the next time I saw her, it would be in a house full of guests that would prevent anything from happening between us.

Or so, you know, I thought...

Twelve

Wynn

"I think this one would be amazing," Perry declared, pulling one of the dresses off the back of the door where I had them hung.

I'd splurged.

I mean, I probably wasn't going to keep all of them. But when I went into the store, I couldn't pick between the five dresses I'd tried on. But Perry hadn't been available to consult. So, naturally, I bought them and waited for her to get a few spare moments to come over and look them over.

"You don't think it's a little... risqué?" I asked, looking at the simple black dress with a fairly modest hemline, but the kind of bodice that could show a lot more than intended.

"When have you ever shied away from something just because it was risqué?" she asked. "Remember that figure drawing class you took. All those penises," she said, giving me a bemused smile.

"It was difficult to get them right on the page since, you know... guys," I said, laughing a bit at the memory of all those dicks getting hard and soft again. Over and over and over. They must have all had blue balls by the time they left the room.

I would never tell Perry this, but that class had given me the experience to be able to do my own private little drawing of a certain cock that belonged to a rich, stupidly handsome, scorchingly sexy boss of mine.

I don't even know what came over me that made me do it. But I'd come home from his house, locked myself in my studio, and started tearing through paper like crazy.

There was a close-up of his perfect cock—thick, long, with shaved balls and a shapely head, then one of him leaned forward in his chair after he'd come down my throat, and one of a woman sucking a man off behind his desk while a shadowy figure stood in the doorway. There was another still of his strong hand fisted in my hair. I liked that one the most. The combination of the silky feminine hair in a strong, masculine grip.

After I finally left my studio, I'd burned through a set of batteries at the memory of going down on him, of the power I'd felt taking him in my mouth, hearing the way my mouth tore away all his defenses, leaving him spent and weak afterward.

As if that in and of itself wasn't hot enough, there was the fact that he'd let me continue to suck him, hidden out of sight, while he attempted to carry on a normal conversation.

We could have been caught.

And that was a fact that sent me shooting through four orgasms until I was too exhausted to continue, and fell into a deep, dreamless sleep.

"Ohhh, wait. What is this?" Perry asked, putting down the one black dress to pick up another.

"Oh, that was kind of just... an impulse buy," I admitted. It had a modest bodice and hem, but a slit that went up pretty high on the thigh.

"This is really neat," she said, running her hand up the black material, which made a golden underside appear.

Admittedly, I'd bought it because I knew that if Fitz put his hand on me anywhere, that it would actually leave a mark on me, and finding myself obsessed with the idea.

"You don't think it is tacky?" I asked. "You know, for a formal affair with a bunch of uber-rich people in attendance?"

"I don't think it is tacky at all. It is perfect."

I'd been secretly hoping that she would pick that one as well. But I needed the objective second set of eyes to make me feel comfortable with the choice.

"Alright. What about shoes?" I asked, waving toward the boxes.

"Well, there will be painful blisters no matter what. My advice is to pick the pair you like so much that you will think the blisters are worth it."

"I like the way you think," I declared.

"So, you're really liking the job, huh?" Perry asked, coming to sit on the bed next to me.

I was definitely starting to really like my boss, that was for sure.

But I couldn't admit that.

"I am. It's been good work," I admitted. "It keeps me engaged, but not super stressed. Well, the party has been a little stressful. But only because of the lack of notice."

"Have you had time to work on your art, though? You are always working lately."

To a fellow creative like Perry, making sure there was always time for your craft was paramount to a happy life. It was why she never managed to hold onto a job, why she quit the moment they didn't give her as much freedom as she needed to go to auditions or do plays.

"I have been working so much lately, actually," I admitted. "I come home, and I end up working for hours. I'm not ready to share it yet," I added, stomach tightening at the idea of Perry seeing my raunchier work.

"You know I would never ask," Perry said, pressing a hand to her heart. "That is very personal. When or if you are ready, I will be eager to see the new work, though."

"I love that about you," I told her. "So, how has work been for you?"

"I have an audition for, believe it or not, a soap."

"You don't sound excited."

"Soaps aren't as big as they used to be. Well, some of them have had pretty decent increases lately, though."

"Well, no one says you need to stay on it until the end of time. Think of how many of today's biggest stars got their start on a soap opera. I mean, if you think about it, what better way to get experience? It is a daily show. And within a year on cast, you would likely have to have three separate star-crossed relationships, several enemies, some sort of health or natural disaster emergency, a faked death, and a dramatic return."

"You seem to know a lot about soaps," Perry said, small eyeing me.

"Okay. It's a guilty pleasure of mine, but I started watching one when I was home sick with the flu as a teen, and I still tune in here and there. There's really nothing else on TV as immersive as a world that has been going for like seventy years, and is on the air five days a week most weeks of the year."

"I can't believe I didn't know this about you."

"I wasn't sure how you would feel about soaps."

"Oh my God, Wynn, you know I would never judge you for what you are into," she said. "Well, except for avocados. Because I am judging you harshly for liking those. You know what I heard about them recently?"

"I don't think I want to."

"That they taste like clean dick."

"Well," I said, mouth falling open. "That... that's... goddamnit, Perry. Now I can't eat them anymore."

"I mean, hey, maybe you like the taste of clean dick," she said, beaming. "But just know that I will be thinking that whenever I see you having some on toast."

"Are you sure you have to go?" I griped, realizing how much I'd missed her lately. We'd both been so busy with work, and then working on our passion projects. We texted and did video calls, but it wasn't the same. "We could order lots of Italian and eat until we are bitching about feeling sick, then eat some more."

"That sounds amazing. But I have my audition. And you need to fit in that amazing dress. But next weekend? We are doing it," she declared as she climbed back off the bed. "Tell me how the party goes, okay?"

"Absolutely. And I want to be your first call after your audition, no matter how it goes."

"You are always my first call," she told me with a big smile as she made her way out of my room.

Alone, I picked out my shoes, and hung the dress on the back of my bedroom door where I could look at and fret about it until it was time to put it on.

And put it on I did.

But not at home.

I'd gone to Fitz's house early to meet all the staff for the party, doing so in ballet flats and a simple pair of slacks and a button-up.

"You're not dressed," Fitz declared as he came down the staircase about an hour or so before the event, still slipping on his cufflinks.

"I've been running around. I have my dress. I just need a minute to get changed."

"I can handle whatever is left," he told me, waving around at the house that looked even cleaner than usual. There was the hustle and bustle of the band, caterers, and servers, but everything was calm and collected chaos.

"You're sure?" I asked, anxious about one of the balls I'd been juggling falling, and potentially ruining the whole event.

"Absolutely. Go up and unwind for a few minutes, then get dressed," Fitz invited.

Whether he knew it or not, a thrill moved through me at his words. Because I knew exactly what kind of unwinding I wanted to do.

"Wynn..." he groaned, letting out a deep sigh.

"Yes?" I asked, tone innocent.

"Don't," he demanded, sounding tense.

"Don't what?" I asked, head tipping to the side.

"You know what," he said, brow raising.

To that, I let a wicked smile tug at my lips. "Don't watch if you don't like it," I suggested, moving past him, making sure to brush him just enough that it could seem like an accident.

So I grabbed my dress, shoes, and small makeup bag, and made my way upstairs.

There were many rooms for me to get ready in. But I walked my ass right into Fitz's room, laying my dress out on the bed, then brought my makeup with me into the bathroom.

Where I did what I'd dreamed about more than a few times in the past. I drew a bath in that amazing tub of his.

Wrapping my hair up to keep it dry, I turned toward the camera, making sure it was positioned toward the tub, then started to strip out of my clothes.

With anticipation sparking off every nerve ending, I slipped under the hot water, feeling it ease the tension in all my muscles. My head tilted toward the camera as my hands started to move over my body, teasing over my breasts, sliding down my belly, then slipping between my thighs.

I knew that Fitz was in the house somewhere watching. In his study, trying to watch in private while people bounced around to get the party ready. Or maybe closed up in a bathroom or spare bedroom, watching on his phone as I brought myself up and through an orgasm, wasting no time since we didn't have it, but needing the release.

Did he get a release too?

Had he jerked off while watching me?

Or had he needed to fight through the desire, deal with a painful erection after I was done?

Either scenario filled me with pleasure as I got out of the bath, as I carefully applied my makeup, styled my hair, and then slipped into the dress.

Perry had been right.

It was the perfect choice.

It hugged my curves, but in a subtle way that didn't make it seem like I intended to be sexy.

I stood there for a moment, toying with the material, watching the way the gold appeared and disappeared when I ran my hand over it.

Then, finally, as I heard the first set of doors opening and closing in the driveway, I spritzed on a little perfume, slipped into my shoes, and made my way toward the stairs.

That was where I found Fitz, greeting his first guests with handshakes and hand claps on shoulders, offering them smiles that didn't come frequently to him.

He was just turning to invite the men into the living room where the band and drinks were set up when his gaze lifted, and he saw me.

I swear, the look on his face right then damn near knocked my breath out of me. There was a fluttering in my chest at the way his hungry gaze slid over me, settling on my face with something that resembled awe in his eyes.

"And who is this?" one of the men there asked. The two of them were non distinct in the looks department. Just two men in their forties with very average builds and bone structure that suggested they were related.

I knew his kind immediately. The kind of rich guy who thought his power and position in life somehow made his leering glances and roving hands less creepy. He was a walking sexual harassment case in the making.

It was something other men tended not to notice, or not acknowledge, but as I made my way down the stairs, knowing I couldn't be rude, Fitz stiffened as he eyed his clients or business partners or whoever they were.

"Robert, Mack, this is my house manager, Wynn. Wynn, Robert and Mack Cloyton."

"House manager," Robert said, offering me his hand, and I had no choice but to shake it. "That is an interesting job title. What does such a job entail?"

I could hear the innuendo in his tone. And despite it being true that I'd been messing around with Fitz, I didn't like the suggestion. Like the only use I served in the household was spread thighs and an open mouth.

"Wynn oversees the rest of the staff, does the household shopping, plans events, and generally makes it possible for me to focus on work," Fitz informed the men before I got a chance to figure out how to explain.

"Interesting," Robert said. "Sounds like something I could use. Do you have any spare time for more work, Wynn?" he asked, and I swore I needed a shower to wipe off the slime his words left all over me.

"I'm afraid I keep her busy," Fitz said. "And she works on her art in her free time."

I didn't intend to have my head whip over to watch his profile, but I couldn't help it. I was a little surprised he even remembered that about me, let alone acknowledged that I spent a chunk of my time working on it. I'd been less than thrilled to find out that most people figured that being an artist meant I scribbled in notebook margins, or could whip out a human-sized canvas in a couple of hours. It was rare to find someone who actually took not only art but the artist and the process seriously.

"Shame. That is a shame," Robert said, shaking his head as his eyes dipped to my chest.

"There is a full bar in the living room, gentlemen," I announced, offering up a tight smile as I waved an arm toward the room. It was a civil dismissal, one they couldn't turn down, so they shuffled off to go get drinks that would likely make Robert even more slimy as the night went on. I made a mental note to avoid him.

"They were... charming," I drawled when they were gone and Fitz and I were alone.

"They're the CFO and CMO of the company I am attempting to buy."

"Attempting?" I asked, waving a hand around his home. "It looks to me like you could afford it."

"It's more that it is an old family business. And the CEO is having a hard time handing it over."

"So you're schmoozing him."

"Something like that," Fitz agreed. "You might want to avoid Robert after he ties on a few," he told me, shaking his head.

"I have already made that mental note. I have no interest in getting groped," I told him, purposely, and very slowly, running a hand across the highest part of my stomach, just under my breasts, turning the black fabric gold.

"Fuck," Fitz hissed under his breath, almost too low to hear. "That's an interesting dress," he said more loudly.

"Isn't it?" I asked. "Try it," I suggested.

"No," he said, and I watched as his hands actually balled into fists like he was struggling to keep himself from doing it.

"What's the matter?" I asked. "Don't trust yourself?"

"Wynn..."

"Just imagine," I started, shooting him a sultry smirk, "me walking around all night with your hand mark on my dress."

"For fuck's sake, Wynn," Fitz said, exhaling hard.

"Were you watching me in your tub?" I asked, knowing from the fire in his eyes that he had. "I figured you would have been dying to touch me—*my* dress," I said.

"I'm not touching you again, Wynn." I'm sure he intended that to sound more firm than it came out.

"Oh, but you want to, don't you?" I asked, turning to face him. "It's killing you not too."

"You need to stop," he said, voice more of a groan than a demand.

"Oh, saved by the bell," I said when the doorbell chimed. "I will see you around, Mr. Buchanan," I added, flipping the gold back to black, loving the way his gaze was glued to the movement until I turned and walked away.

Within half an hour, the party was in full swing.

There were about twenty guests, all in all, plus the staff that moved around with the calm, but purposeful efficiency that came with experience with these sorts of events.

Meanwhile, I felt completely out of place.

I was an outsider who was forced to be on the inside. Which made me hug the walls, and make pleasant but superficial conversations with anyone who would speak to me, so I didn't feel quite so awkward.

Then, about an hour and a half into the event, it happened.

The slimy jerk snuck up on me.

With that thing old men who felt entitled to your body did.

He put his hand low on my back, so low that his little finger was actually resting at the curve of my ass.

Damnit.

I'd been keeping such a close eye on him, ducking out and heading to the kitchen when he seemed to be trying to move closer to me.

"I've been trying to catch you all night," he said, whiskey breath near my ear.

"I must be very slippery," I said, stomach tightening.

"Yes, well, I've got you now," he said, his other hand moving to grab my hip, pulling my body closer to his.

Now, I'd been cornered by a man more than once in my life. I'd had unwanted hands on me. I'd felt that sick, rolling sensation in my stomach. But in those other situations, I'd been able to be loud and rude to get away, or to alert someone else to come and help me.

I didn't have that luxury in this situation.

The reasons were obvious.

This was someone my boss had been courting—in the business sense—for months. I was just the house help. If I was rude to Robert, Fitz would have needed to take a stand with him in the situation if he hoped to save the buyout.

"Mr. Cloyton," I started, trying to take a step back, which only made his fingers sink in deeper.

"I like how my name sounds on those pretty lips," he said, making me feel a little queasy.

"Wynn," Fitz's voice called, sounding tight. "Can I see you in the kitchen for a moment?" he asked. "There's an issue with the caterer," he added, giving me the out I so desperately needed.

Robert had no choice but to release me, but not before telling me he would find me later. It sounded more like a threat than a promise.

I scurried away out of the living room, only to be snagged by Fitz as I almost rushed past him without seeing him. His hand grabbed my wrist, pulling me with him up the back staircase for privacy.

"You okay?" he asked, looking down at my face that must have been flushed because it felt hot.

"Ugh. Yeah. He's a complete asshole," I declared, waving down at my dress, then doing a little circle so he could see the spots where Robert had put his hands on me.

A growling noise moved through Fitz as he reached out again, but this time not to grab me.

Oh, no.

His hand drifted down my side, over my hip, then around my lower back, making all the gold from Robert's hands disappear.

"I'm sorry."

"It's not your fault. How were you supposed to know he was a groper unless you saw it in action?" I asked.

"I made you be here," he added, his hand finished erasing, but getting busy making his own marks with the whisper-soft tips of his fingers. "You've been uncomfortable all night."

"You noticed?" I asked, gaze on his face since his was downcast, watching his fingers create patterns in my dress.

"Of course I noticed," he said, his voice a low, smooth sound that washed over my skin, making a shiver move through me. "I just couldn't get away."

"You wanted to?" I asked, needing to hear the words from him.

"Couldn't keep my mind on anything else since you walked down the stairs in this dress," he told me, fingers gliding up my belly to tease across the underside of my breasts.

"You like it?" I asked, dropping my voice a bit lower too. At that, his gaze cut to mine, showing me heavy lids and molten eyes. "Did you get a good look at the whole thing?" I asked, turning ever so slowly until my back was just barely brushing his chest.

"Wynn..."

There was next to no control in his voice right then.

Which was exactly how I wanted him.

"Did you see this?" I added, covering his hand with mine and guiding it down my belly, over my hip, then down my thigh, sliding inward to find the slit, then gliding it up my bare leg.

An actual growling sound escaped Fitz then as his fingers curled in for a moment like he was trying to keep them from moving, his fingernails biting crescents into my flesh.

He lost the battle, though, and his hand flattened and started moving up.

"I didn't see you put panties on," he mumbled in my ear as I leaned back against him.

"That's because I didn't," I told him, turning my head in toward his neck, taking a deep breath of his spicy cologne. "I didn't put a bra on either," I told him, taking his other hand from its placement just above my hip, and putting it over my breast, forcing it to curl in, to squeeze the soft flesh.

A low moan moved through me as I released his hand, raising my arm up and back, grasping the back of his neck, giving him full access to me.

There was the briefest of pauses before he lost his battle with himself, and his hand was sliding upward, slipping under the neckline of my bodice, closing over my bare breast in such a hard, possessive way that a surge of need pooled between my thighs at the contact.

My ass wiggled backward against Fitz, feeling the proof of his desire pressing against me.

A whimper moved out of me as Fitz's fingers went to my nipple, rolling it into a tightened bud before pinching, squeezing, then moving across my chest.

"We have to stop," he murmured as I wiggled my ass against his erection.

"I can't imagine why."

"I have a house full of guests."

"They're being wined and fed. They don't even realize you're gone."

"Someone could see us," he said. And despite his words to the contrary, his hand on my thigh moved higher still, teasing the skin there, but not quite making the contact I so desperately needed.

"Oh, but doesn't that make it all the more exciting?" I asked, arching upward, so when my hips slipped down again, his cock pressed between my thighs.

"Wynn..."

"Just say yes," I demanded, leaning in to press a kiss to his throat. "We both want it," I added, wiggling against him. And the motion made his hand slip.

"Fuck, you're so wet," he groaned as his fingers seemed helpless but to slide up my cleft, to tease around my clit.

"See how much I need you?" I asked as his finger moved down and slipped inside me. "I want you inside me," I added as his fingers started to fuck me.

I knew by the sound of his growl that he was too far gone to fight it anymore.

I turned in his arms, wrapping my arms around his neck, and sealing my lips to his.

If I'd been expecting hesitation, I found none as his lips crushed to mine, deepening the kiss, demanding more, everything.

His teeth nipped my lower lip, dragging a ragged moan from me that allowed his tongue to move inside and claim mine.

His hand roamed over my back, my ass, then slipped back between my thighs, driving me up toward that fever pitch.

"Fitz, fuck me," I demanded as my hands went between us to work his button and zipper free.

On a growl, his hands moved down to snag the material of my dress, starting to slowly pull the skirt upward, bunching in his hands even as my hand grabbed his cock, pulling it out, and stroking him.

"Fuck," he growled as my finger stroked over the head, making a shiver course through him. "Back pocket," he said, voice rough.

My hand slid around his hip, sinking into his ass for a second before fetching his wallet out of his back pocket, then searching blindly for the foil.

"Here," he said as I found it and tucked his wallet away again.

"I've got it," I told him, watching the heat in his eyes for another second as I stroked him before opening the condom, and sliding it on.

As soon as I was done, he turned us, slamming me back against the wall, reached down to grab my thigh, pulled it up, and spread it wide against the wall as he stepped inward.

His cock pressed between my thighs, slipping up and down my slick cleft, then tapping on my clit until I was writhing and begging for more.

"Fitz, please," I begged, wiggling my hips against him.

Before I could even draw in a steadying breath, his cock was surging inside me, making me take every thick inch of him as he buried to the hilt.

A choked moan escaped me as my forehead pressed into his shoulder as I was overcame with the strangest set of sensations. The only way I could describe it was, it felt right.

I couldn't think of a single time that had ever been on my mind.

Sure, sex was usually good, something I wanted. But I'd never felt such a strong and immediate connection as I did right then.

"Wynn," Fitz called, pulling me out of my confusing thoughts and feelings as I leaned back against the wall, angling my head up to look at him. "There you are," he said as his free hand settled at the side of my throat as his cock slid out then surged back in. Slow, measured. And he seemed to take a lot of pleasure in watching my reaction to his surprisingly patient movements. "You're so fucking tight," he growled as he started to thrust faster, losing his tight grip on his control.

My arms went around the back of his neck, pulling him down toward me, muffling my moans with his lips as he fucked me harder and harder still.

"Come," he demanded as he felt my pussy clench hard around him as I teetered on that edge for a long moment before getting pushed over it, crashing down into my orgasm. "Fuck," he hissed, fucking me through it, drawing it out. But when I came back down, he was still hard inside me, still aching for more.

When my gaze found his again, he grabbed me, turned me, and pressed me forward, forcing me to grab the very top of the banister over the floor below.

Someone could pass by and look up at any time.
I was rubbing off on him.
But before I could relish that fact, he was fisting my skirt at my lower back and slamming inside me.

Hard.

Deep.

He dropped my skirt, his hands grabbing my hips instead, using them to slam me back against him as he thrust forward, forcing me to take each thick inch of him.

There was nothing slow or explorative of him right them.

He fucked me hard and fast, the sounds of our bodies slamming together rivaling the band in the living room below.

"That's it, squeeze my cock," he hissed as he pushed me to that edge, then tossed me over before I could even prepare for it. "More," he demanded as I just barely managed to keep a cry inside me as the final waves crashed through my system.

"I... can't," I whimpered, all my nerve endings feeling shot, leaving me frazzled and overstimulated.

"You're going to," he told me, releasing my hips to grab a handful of my hair with one hand, the pain blooming across my scalp with each thrust as he continued to fuck me, harder even than before.

His other hand moved forward, yanking down my bodice in the front, exposing my breasts to the air, to anyone below, to whoever might be driving past out the big foyer window.

Fitz's gaze was pinned on our reflection in that window as he fucked me, making my tits bounce.

His hand grabbed one of my breasts, squeezing for a moment before moving downward to slip between my thighs, engaging my clit, and proving to me that he was right.

I was going to come again.

"I'm going to come," I moaned, wiggling my hips in circles as he fucked me so hard, I was genuinely concerned we might both surge forward over the banister and fall to the foyer floor below.

"Yeah, you are," he agreed as my pussy tightened around him.

"Oh my God," I cried as he got me closer and closer. "Fitz," I moaned.

And just like that, his cock slammed forward as his finger swiped my clit.

And I fucking shattered.

I splintered all around.

My cry was a loud, uninhibited sound that ricocheted off the walls.

Before I could even realize what was happening, Fitz was dragging me backward with him away from the banister, knowing my cries would draw someone's attention.

Back in the relative privacy of the hallway, his hands grabbed my shoulders, holding me in place as he fucked me faster and faster as his body tensed, as he got close.

And when he came?

Yeah, it was my name on his lips.

Again, I was overwhelmed with that feeling of rightness even as I came back down from my orgasm, leaving me shaky and weak, and somehow both hot and cold at the same time.

"Christ," Fitz hissed as he pulled me back against his back, his arms going around me—one above my breasts, just under my clavicles, the other low on my hips.

Tight.

Possessive.

And, God, did I like that.

I shouldn't have.

It didn't make sense.

I liked the thrill of the chase. I got off on having a man want me, but not be able to have me. I didn't get all warm and fuzzy over a man who had me, who seemed to want to hold onto me. That wasn't how I was wired.

Or, perhaps, I'd just never found the right man in the past.

The right man?

No.

I didn't want that. I wasn't looking for that. And Fitzwilliam Buchanan was the last person I could ever have that with.

I could feel myself recoiling from that thought. Which was why I forced my brain to repeat it over and over until it had me stiffening and pulling out of his hold.

"You have guests," I reminded him, wincing a bit at the sharp edge to my words as I moved away completely, straightening my dress and tucking my breasts away again before turning to face him again.

And there he was, head ducked to the side a bit, watching me with a quizzical brow.

"What's the matter?" he asked, refusing to just let me have my confusion in peace.

"Nothing," I said, lifting my chin a bit, trying to give the impression of honesty through the lie. "But there is going to be something the matter if you don't get back down there and kiss-ass with your business partners," I added, making my tone a little higher, lighter, but it sounded painfully fake even to my own ears.

"Wynn..." he said, his arm moving.

I knew that if I let him reach out to me right then, it was not going to be good for me in the long term. I needed to keep my distance right then. I was feeling too raw and vulnerable, too mixed up in my own head and heart. I needed some time and space to get myself together.

"I need to go... freshen up," I said, waving at my hair that had to have been askew from his hands. "I'll see you down there."

With that, I turned and all but ran away from him.

And the growing feelings there was no denying I was starting to feel for him.

Thirteen

Fitz

She'd been true to her word.

At least partially.

I did "see her down there" after she spent half an hour freshening up.

I wasn't sure what kind of freshening up she'd done, but when she'd made it back downstairs after, there was something cold and untouchable about her. In fact, she'd even smoothed away the golden traces of my touch from her dress. Front and back.

Like she was trying to erase what had happened.

But, no. That made no sense. She'd initiated it. Since the beginning, she'd always been the one to initiate. Hell, she'd literally asked for it, demanded I fuck her right there in full display of anyone who might happen through the foyer.

Damn if it hadn't been the best fucking sex of my life too.

So much so that my cock got half hard anytime I spotted her or even smelled her scent in the air if she passed by.

The thing was, she'd made it a point to avoid being anywhere near me for the rest of the evening. She'd spent all her time engaging the wives who'd come, then dipping off to the kitchen or talking to the servers, all the while avoiding Robert.

And me.

I'd just gotten close enough at one point to reach out, to pull her into the hallway to demand to know what was going on when my damn brother came bursting in, already half drunk with a girl who hadn't even attempted to go for classy with the bright pink dress with hipbone cutouts.

I couldn't look away from Blake or his date for the rest of the evening, lest they do or say something that would compromise the deal. Hell, just having them there was embarrassing enough. I needed to make sure they didn't make it any worse than it was.

But because of that, Wynn had somehow managed not only to disappear from the crowd, but hide out somewhere even after it dispersed.

She'd stuck behind until all the staff had left. But before I could uncover her hiding spot, I caught sight of her tail lights as she pulled out of the driveway.

I should have been exhausted. True, Wynn had handled all the preparation for the event, but I wasn't a party person by nature. So all the socializing had been foreign and draining.

Any other time, I would have fallen into bed immediately after, sleeping it off.

Instead, though, I found myself sitting in my study with a drink in my hand, trying to figure out what the hell had happened with Wynn.

That was another first for me. I'd never been someone who analyzed their interaction with the opposite sex. I always accepted it at face value. Good, bad, or indifferent. There was never any reason to analyze it because it never meant anything.

This shouldn't have meant anything either.

But, somehow, I guess it did.

I wanted to tell myself it was just because we'd been explosive with each other, that I'd never felt that exhilarated before, had never come so hard in my life.

But after two drinks, I dragged myself up to my bedroom, stripping out of clothes that still had her scent all over them, and dropping into bed with one realization: it wasn't about the sex.

I mean, sure, it was a factor. Sex was always a factor. If you were having it, if you weren't, it was always something to consider. But sex wasn't the only reason I couldn't get her out of my head, was it?

There was some sort of connection between us, something that was both exciting yet comfortable at the same time.

I'd been a lifelong workaholic. I'd always felt more comfortable at the office than at home. Somehow, though, knowing Wynn was there gave me something to look forward to. I'd been cutting workdays short several times a week since she'd started to work for me.

I told myself that it was just because I wanted to watch the cameras, see what show she was putting on for me. There was that, of course. I won't deny it. I did a lot of thinking with my dick when it came to Wynn. It was more than that, though. The house felt more comfortable with her there. It had been surprisingly nice to have someone to talk to, even about banal house shit, or even to listen to her rib me relentlessly about the art in the house.

I'd never shared my life or home with a woman before.

I liked it more than I had any right to.

Especially since she didn't belong to me.

I didn't want anyone to belong to me.

And certainly not one of my employees.

The thing was, though, I'd been reconsidering my feelings on that last point sometime between the pool and the balcony in the foyer.

Sure, the sex was good. And, in my opinion, good sex was a worthy pursuit in life.

But it was more than that.

And I wanted it to continue to be more than that.

I guess I never considered the fact that maybe Wynn didn't feel the same way.

But after the third workday passed after the party with her managing to somehow avoid me at every turn, no matter how relentlessly I tried to catch her for a minute, I guess there was no denying that she was absolutely avoiding me.

But why?

Because she regretted what we'd done?

Or because she was done with me once we'd done it?

Maybe for her it was all about the tease, the chase, the excitement of the lead-up, more so than actually sealing the deal. Once all the teasing and chasing was done, and the orgasms had settled, perhaps it was all over for her. Maybe she wanted to go off to the next conquest.

Unexpectedly, a sharp stabbing sensation pierced my chest at that thought, acute enough to have my hand raising, rubbing at my heart.

"What's the matter, Big Brother, is it shrinking another couple sizes?" Blake asked, waltzing into my study, looking hungover and scruffy. I just barely resisted the urge to ask if he'd gone into work looking like that, knowing it was only going to lead to a fight, and I just didn't have the energy or mental wherewithal to deal with that right then.

"Cute," I said, tone dry, reaching for the envelope he handed me. "What's this?"

"I don't know. Came by courier today. Wynn came to get me to sign for it."

So she would talk to Blake, outwardly seek out Blake, but not me. Her avoidance definitely wasn't all in my mind.

One glance at the label told me all I needed to know.

"Aren't you going to open it?"

"No."

"It's important enough to require a signature, but not to open?"

"Correct."

"Fine," Blake said, sighing. "I'm going out."

"You look like you need to sleep more than have another night out."

Shit.

I regretted it the second it was out of my mouth.

Because within three minutes, as usual, we were all but screaming at each other.

It never took much for us to get to the point of raised voices and dredging up old shit. It didn't matter how many times we'd done it, or how much resentment old arguments had already put upon our relationship. We just didn't seem capable of being calm and rational with each other.

"For God's sake," another voice joined, raised to be heard over ours. "Are you serious right now? Wynn added, standing in the doorway to the study with her hands fisted on her hips. "You sound like a couple of squabbling five-year-olds. You're grown-ass men, for chrissakes. Act like it. The whole damn neighborhood can hear you hauling insults at each other."

"Squabbling," Blake repeated, rolling the word around in his mouth. He'd always been able to bring his anger from one-hundred down to one much faster than I could. "You don't hear that word much anymore. It's a good word."

"Yeah, it's much nicer than 'coldhearted dickhead,' don't you think?" she asked, tone pointed, brow arched.

"I have a... colorful vocabulary," Blake said, giving her one of his boyish smiles that made me want to reach out and slap it off his face. Because it always allowed him to get away with anything he wanted.

I was taking special exception to the way he was using it on Wynn.

Apparently, though, Wynn was more immune to it than others.

"No, Blake. That isn't a colorful vocabulary. It's name-calling. And it's the sign of a weak argument."

"Or is it a crude observation of an undeniable truth?" Blake shot back, talking about me like I wasn't standing right fucking there.

"I think it is proof that you and your brother have some issues you clearly need to work on. With some sort of impartial mediator," Wynn said, shaking her head at him. "All of this is unproductive. I'm sure you have other things you'd rather be doing than arguing what I can only assume is the same old argument with your brother."

"You are right about that," Blake said, nodding. "Lots of pretty ladies out there I could be making smile instead. Care to go get a drink and be one of them?" he asked.

I hoped to hell the growl I let out at his words wasn't loud enough for either of them to hear from across the room. There was no denying to myself, however, that was exactly what it was. A growl. A base, primal sound brought about by the prospect of Wynn spending her free time with my brother.

I'd never been a possessive man before. I'd never cared enough about a woman to be upset when her free time wasn't saved for me.

I guess that was further proof that I didn't just want to keep fucking Wynn. I wanted something more than that.

"I can't."

"Hot date?" Blake asked.

It was a throwaway kind of question, but I felt my stomach twisting for a long second before she answered.

"Yes, with my paintbrush and a fresh canvas."

"Oh, right. I forgot you play around with art in your free time."

Well, if I'd been worrying Wynn might transfer her interest from me to the much more laid-back and fun Blake, it all slipped away with that comment. As well as her reaction to it.

Her eyes blazed bright enough to damn near scorch me from across the room. Her jaw tightened. Her chin raised. And her arms crossed over her chest.

If you wanted to piss off a creative person, implying that their craft was something to be fiddled with in their free time after working at their 'real job' was a pretty damn good way to do it.

Wynn looked two seconds away from starting an argument with Blake that would rival the one I'd just had with him.

"Blake, I think you are going to want to shut your mouth and leave," I suggested even as he seemed to notice the same thing about Wynn that I did right then.

"Right. Yeah. I, you know, didn't mean anything," he said, rushing out.

"You never do," I grumbled to myself even as my gaze fell on Wynn again, practically shaking in her rage.

"He's an idiot who doesn't think before he speaks," I told her, watching as her gaze cut to me. "I can't apologize for his ignorance, but he doesn't speak for the whole family," I added. "I know your art is an important part of your life, and that the time you dedicate to it is valid."

At that, she took a slow, deep breath, and exhaled it on a sigh as her arms fell down at her sides.

"Thank you. I know it shouldn't get a rise out of me. I've been hearing it all my life that art isn't a 'real job.' And, I guess, for most of us, it isn't. We tend to have to go out and get jobs that will pay the bills."

"I'm sure you will make a name for yourself in due time," I told her. She was smart and dedicated. If she set her mind to succeeding, I didn't doubt she would get there eventually. No matter the odds. "Whenever there is a rule, there are exceptions to it."

"That's true," she agreed, relaxing by the second. "And Blake might be a nice enough guy, but..." she started, trailing off as she waved a hand outward.

"He has absolutely no idea how the world works? Yeah, I'm painfully aware of that fact."

"Can I ask you something?"

"Of course."

"Why do you take care of him? I know it might be a cultural thing, but in the middle or even upper-middle class, when you have an irresponsible ingrate, the caretakers tend to cut them off eventually, so they get a chance to get a kick in the ass that will set them on the right path."

"It's our father," I told her, shrugging. "He asked me to look after Blake."

"I understand that. But would your father insist that to do that, you would need to put up with the disrespect he always gives you?"

"You have a point," I admitted. "My father was more tolerant of Blake's behavior than he would have been with me. I think age softens parenting styles. But he would never have put up with the way Blake destroys the house." *Amongst other things.*

"I mean, I'm not saying you should cut him out of your life, or off completely. But maybe if he had to learn how much things actually cost because he has to pay his own rent, utilities, food, and furnishing costs, he would be more considerate."

"You're not wrong," I agreed.

"But it's hard," she concluded for me.

"It probably shouldn't be, considering all he's done. But yes."

"Maybe because you still see him as your little brother instead of a full-grown man."

"Again, you're not wrong," I agreed.

"It's probably easier for me to say it than for you to act on it. I'm an only child. I don't fully understand the sibling dynamic."

"It's a tough one to explain," I admitted. "I spend eighty-percent of my time arguing with him or being pissed at him, but I can't shake the attachment either."

"That's... unexpectedly sweet, though."

"I'm not a complete asshole," I said, tensing.

"I never said you were."

"I know you see me as cold and—"

"You don't know what I think about you," she cut me off, shaking her head.

"I'm coming to conclusions since you seem to be avoiding me like I've contracted the plague."

"I'm working," she countered, but I thought it was telling that she didn't say she wasn't avoiding me.

"Must be more difficult work than usual," I observed. "Your usual uniform has changed."

Gone were the dresses and skirts that could easily slide up. She'd been wearing slacks since the party. High-waisted slacks with tucked in button-up shirts that she actually buttoned all the way up. And wore a bra under just for added concealment.

"It's been really cold out," she told me.

And, to be fair, she wasn't lying. December's freeze had come on hard and fast, plummeting the average daily temperatures to an average of thirty, with colder nights and mornings.

"Oh, speaking of that," I said, though it was a weak segue at best. Moving around my desk, I went into the top drawer to pull out a new key fob. I spun it around my finger before tossing it toward her.

She caught it with drawn together brows. "What's this? Do you need your car washed?" she asked.

"No. That is the key to the car I want you to use."

"Wait... what?" she asked, looking more confused than before.

"No offense, Wynn, but I swear your car was hacking up a lung last night. You need to be driving something reliable if you are going to be able to get your work done around here."

"Oh, okay. So I will drive this when I run the errands, and just save gas receipts for you?" she asked.

"You will drive it to and from work as well."

"What? No."

"Yes. If your car finally craps out on you when you need to be here to oversee something being done, there will be a problem. Drive this car instead. And, yes, save the gas receipts."

"And mileage reports," she muttered.

"No. I don't give a shit about the mileage."

"But what if I used it for personal use?" she asked, rolling her eyes.

"Again, I don't give a shit about that. It's just a car."

"Just a..." she started, her gaze going down to the fob, seeing the logo there. "This is not *just a car*."

"Sure it is."

"This is a touchscreen key fob. I can't imagine how expensive the car that goes with this is."

"Wynn, it's just a car."

"What if I crash it? Or dent it with a shopping cart?" she asked, eyes big.

"Then I will fix it."

"That's ridiculous."

"What's ridiculous is that we're arguing over this," I countered.

"This isn't an argument. This is me informing you that I can't be driving around a luxury car."

"Why not?"

"Because... because it isn't mine."

"It is yours in everything but the actual title. I don't see the problem."

And I won't have to worry about you freezing on your way to and from my house anymore, either.

Not that it was appropriate to think about shit like that when it came to an employee. But, then again, there was a lot that was inappropriate about what went on with Wynn and me.

Or, at least, there had been.

"I..." Wynn started, not sure what she was going to say, but wanting to object.

"It's not a big deal."

"What if it gets stripped? I don't live in the nicest area."

There was a twisting sensation in my gut at her words. I couldn't help but picture her in some crummy apartment in some bad area of town with unsavory sorts waiting in dark alleys to reach out to her.

I had the most irrational urge to demand she move into the guest room. Hell, into my goddamn bedroom.

What the hell was going on with me?

"I won't hold you responsible."

"I, ah, I'm going to need to see that in writing," Wynn declared, giving me a nod.

"That will ease your mind?"

"Yes."

"Fine," I said, grabbing my notepad and pen. "'*Wynn is in no way responsible for any damage or mileage that might happen to the car I have given to her to use while she is under my employ. Signed Fitzwilliam Buchanan.* Good enough?"

"I think it isn't binding unless it's notarized."

"You're serious?" I asked, a laugh escaping me.

"Kinda, yeah."

"Alright. I will get it notarized on my way to work tomorrow."

"Good."

"So, you'll drive it."

"Well, not tonight."

"Why not?"

"Because I have my car here," she said, shrugging.

"I will get it towed back to your place."

"What? No."

"It's done," I said, already reaching for the phone.

"Um, no. No, it's not done."

"Hi, yes. I need my car towed," I said into my phone, cutting off her objection. She stood there in pensive silence as I finished the phone call. "There," I declared when I was done. "All handled. Happy?"

"I don't understand," Wynn admitted.

"It's not complicated. You have a more reliable car to drive, so I can depend on you to continue to do your job to my satisfaction."

"But..."

"But nothing."

"Mr. Buchanan—" she started, making a frustrated sigh escape me.

"Mr. Buchanan?" I asked, brow raising in a way that said *Aren't we beyond that?*

"Fitz," she said instead, voice a little airless.

I had her off-kilter.

And I liked it more than I should have, given the situation.

I could probably have approached her then, demanded an explanation for the change in her behavior since we'd had sex. But something inside me said this was the better way to play it. Keep her confused and surprised. I would get more from her that way.

Maybe I'd even get some answers.

Maybe I'd get her to agree to be more than just a fuck-buddy.

What?

No.

I didn't do more than casual encounters.

Even as I tried to remind myself of that fact, though, there was another part of me that was screaming that I wanted more than a few weeks of teasing and one fuck, that I wanted more than the physical in general.

What the hell was that about?

"Are you done for the night?" I asked, hearing the roughness in my tone as my mind went to battle with itself.

"Ah, yeah."

"Head on out. The car is in the first garage," I told her.

"Right," she agreed nodding, then turning, starting to walk away before turning back. "Mr... Fitz," she said, catching herself.

"Yes?"

"Thank you," she said, looking even more confused than before.

"You're welcome."

And with that, she was gone, leaving me with my swirling thoughts to keep me company for the rest of the night.

Hours later, I was no closer to coming to any sort of rational understanding about my confusing feelings for Wynn.

But I did know one thing.

I wanted more.

And I was going to do whatever it took to get that.

Fourteen

Wynn

He gave me a car.
Well, I mean, not technically.
But, also, he had.
It was mine in everything but title, but I didn't have to do anything to pay for it, to maintain it, or even to fuel it up.
It was a black BMW 7-Series with the kind of grill and rims that any casual passerby knew it was

expensive. And after a quick Google search, I nearly choked on my own spit to see a price tag of almost ninety-thousand.

Ninety-Thousand.

For a car.

That he wasn't even going to drive.

I almost marched right back into the house to hand him back the fancy touchscreen key fob before words of much wiser persons than myself crossed my mind.

Don't look a gift horse in the mouth.

Why shouldn't I take it if he was offering it? I had it in writing that nothing that happened to it would impact me.

On that thought, I unlocked the door, opening it to find a fancy tan and black interior that made me think I'd never be able to drink my morning coffee in it on the way to work anymore for fear of staining the buttery smooth leather.

I had the irrational urge to slide off my shoes before I climbed in, but just barely managed to fight it off as I got in, closed the door, and reached for the push ignition, hearing it purr to life.

And, glory of glories, after maybe only two minutes of cold air blasting out of the vents, hot air danced around my face and hair.

"This is like a spaceship," I declared to the car as I eyed the touchscreen command center. "Oh, no way," I gasped, pressing my finger against the screen where it claimed I not only had heated seats, but a heated steering wheel and armrests as well.

Sure enough, within a minute or two, my butt, thighs, arms, and hands were all toasty warm, and I was seriously considering giving up my art dreams to become a venture capitalist or something because, well, I suddenly decided I could not live without heated seats, armrests, and steering wheels for the rest of my life.

On that note, though, I adjusted the seat and mirrors, then hit the button clipped to the visor for the garage, and backed out past my somewhat trusty beater, feeling a bit guilty driving past it in such luxury.

The whole road home, I refused to let my mind wander past enjoying the way nothing rattled and no lights lit up my dashboard.

But after I got home, locked up the fancy new car, and went up into my apartment, there was no stopping the flooding of thoughts that assaulted me all at once.

Fitz got me a car.

I mean, sure, there might have been some rationality to his argument about my car being unreliable, but he'd also never experienced an inconvenience on my part because of my shoddy means of transportation, so it wasn't like that really should have even been on his mind.

So why then?

Because we'd had sex?

Fitz didn't strike me as the sort of man to buy a woman gifts for fucking him. It wasn't like he would have a hard time getting laid. He was rich, handsome, and a pretty nice guy under all the guards he put up.

He didn't need to give women gifts in exchange for their attention and affection.

So why then?

Especially since I'd been freezing him out since the party.

See, after taking off to freshen up and get myself together, I came to the realization that it wasn't safe for me to keep allowing things to be sexual between Fitz and me.

Because I was having confusing thoughts and feelings about him that had nothing to do with sex.

It was risky enough to have a sexual relationship with your boss, but to let one-sided feelings start to get involved? That was a recipe for disaster. It was a surefire way to lose my job as well as the stability I'd started to get accustomed to thanks to it.

So I needed to distance myself. I needed to control my urges to put on a show for the cameras, for the man sitting at his desk watching the feeds from them.

I had to get it together.

I had to put an end to it.

So I put on clothes that wouldn't allow for any sort of malfunctions and I focused my mind on the tasks at hand instead of which angles the cameras were catching me at, and wondering if Fitz was watching me.

It made the days long and boring and exhausting.

But that was what a job was like, right?

On a sigh, I kicked out of my boring flats, took off my bland slacks and button-up, slipped into an oversized tee, and headed into my studio.

Where I stared at the blank canvas until my eyes got blurry.

See, what I'd told Blake was only a half-truth.

I actually hadn't been able to put my paintbrush to a canvas in days.

I blamed my strange mood.

My art flourished with strong emotions like love or hate or anger and joy.

But I felt emotionally stunted right then. Weird and unfocused, my mind whipping from one thing to some completely unrelated thing the next second, leaving me wired and antsy, but too all over the place to get anything onto a canvas or even a damn sketchpad.

I was artistically stuck.

And it was scarier than I could have anticipated, to think I'd lost something that had always been such a vital part of my life.

On a strange whimper, I tossed the brush back into the coffee can I kept them in, and made my way out of the studio to grab my phone.

I didn't call Perry.

I usually would have.

If not for the whole boss thing.

She was understanding and nonjudgmental about most things, but I wasn't sure how she would react to this sort of conversation.

But there was one person I could always count on understanding and never ever judging.

"Hey, honey!" my mom's chipper voice met my ear.

"I can't paint," I said, hearing the mix of desperation and fear in my voice.

"Huh," my mom said as I put water on for hot chocolate. "Okay. Well, what is going on that might be messing up your aura?"

"It's sort of a long story," I admitted, putting a teabag and sugar into a mug as I watched the electric kettle start to warm up.

"And the condensed version is?"

"I, ah, I sort of slept with my boss," I admitted.

"Did he fire you?"

"Ah, no. Actually, he is lending me a really fancy car," I admitted.

"Is he now?"

"It's not a sex gift," I insisted.

"Of course not. I would never imply that, darling. I'm afraid I'm not seeing the issue here. You slept with your boss and he is being kind to you?"

Okay, put like that, it didn't sound all that confusing or complicated.

"I, ah, it was... I sort of... you know... initiated it. But it was really more of a game. For weeks. And then..."

"And then you had sex and decided maybe it isn't just a game to you after all."

My mom, bless her heart. She always got it.

"Exactly."

"And what has happened since then?"

"Well, I, ah, I distanced myself. I can't have feelings for my boss."

"Why not?"

"Because, you know, it's like a rule."

"Whose rule? Is it his rule? Your rule? You are the only two people whose opinions matter on this issue, don't you think?"

"Well... yeah, I guess."

"His opinion seems to be clear."

"I mean, not really. He said I needed a reliable car to keep doing my job."

"My sweet girl, you are not that gullible. I can all but guarantee you that the car has nothing to do with your job. Men don't typically think like that. Right, honey?" she asked, but I knew she wasn't talking to me by the way her voice got far away. "Wynnie wants to know if a boss out of nowhere gets his assistant a fancy new car just so she can do her job more effectively."

"That depends," my step-father said, likely leaning his head against my mothers to talk into her phone. "Has your car been breaking down lately?"

"No. I mean, it does its usual nonsense, but never that he has known about."

"Then no. That is not typical," he said, and I could already tell he'd lost interest in the conversation. I loved my step-father, but he was a practical man who didn't usually have a lot of time for chit-chat. I guess that was why he and my impractical and loquacious mother worked so well.

"See?" my mother asked. "I think your boss might have feelings for you, but doesn't know how to express it. Bill was the same way when we first started dating. He was wholly incapable of telling me he was into me, so he would take my car to get it washed and serviced, or hire someone to come in and fix the leaky sink in my kitchen, or tell me he just so happened to get tickets from a client to a nearly sold-out and very expensive opera I'd told him I was dying to see. Sometimes men weren't raised to regulate and express their feelings, so they show them instead of telling you about them."

"I just... I don't think my boss has feelings for me," I insisted, pouring my hot water into my cup.

"Why not? Because he's rich and powerful and you're not?" my mom asked, making me wince because, to an extent, that was something that had crossed my mind.

"He could have any woman he wanted," I said, knowing it was true.

"Sure, darling. But he wants you. Who are you to tell him he's mistaken in his decision? Those are his feelings to feel, not yours to change. You don't have to participate in his feelings if you don't want to. That's your choice. But it's really not your place to question why he wants you. He just does."

My mother, bless her, was one of the most self-assured people I'd ever met. Not cocky or conceited in any way, just sure of herself, never plagued with rampant intrusive thoughts about her own inadequacy. She didn't question why people adored her, just accepted it.

I, however, didn't inherit that gene.

Sure, I was confident in many ways. In my physicality, in my sexuality, in my talent, in my drive and ambition to make something for myself.

But when it came to things like feelings and relationships? That wasn't my strong suit. The path behind me was littered with the scattered, decaying remains of all my previous relationships. It stretched back to when I first started dating at fifteen and ended about a year ago.

It just never worked.

And it left me with this lingering worry that there was simply something wrong with me that I could never make it work, that no one ever just looked at me and saw me as enough.

These were just average guys, too. Not rich, powerful, educated, and cultured like Fitz.

What would a man like that see in me?

Other than sex, obviously.

Maybe that was what it boiled down to.

I was sure all he could want from me was sex—since I had worked hard at making him want that—and a part of me was terrified that after we'd done it, he would be done with me.

"Listen, Wynnie, I get it. You're struggling to see it right now. I'm just suggesting you be open to letting him show you," my mom suggested.

"That's... that's good advice," I decided.

"I'm known for it," my mom agreed, and I could almost see the smile I knew she had on her face.

"I miss you."

"I miss you too, sweetie. Just a couple more weeks," she assured me.

Schedule-wise, we hadn't been able to swing actual Christmas this year, but we were going to spend a few days together between Christmas and New Years.

"I want some details on you and your boss," she demanded. "If things happen between now and when I see you. I also wouldn't object to a picture of the man who is spoiling my much-deserving little girl."

"I'll see what I can do," I said.

"Good. Don't overthink it. Just let the universe guide you."

"I'll try," I agreed.

"Good. Love you, baby."

"Love you too," I said, ending the call and taking a sip of my tea, deciding she was right.

I had growing feelings.

And if Fitz did too, wasn't that worth exploring?

I would just... take my cues from him.

On that note, I went back into my studio to work, finally getting something done for the first time in days.

—

"What do you mean you don't have a Christmas tree?" I asked, sure I misunderstood him, like perhaps he always got a *real* tree each year, so he didn't have one at the moment.

"I don't have one," Fitz said, shrugging from behind his laptop screen.

"Do you get a real one each year then?" I demanded to know.

"No, I do not," Fitz said, half closing the lid of his laptop, looking over at me with drawn-together brows. "You look insulted," he said, lips twitching.

"Do you... you know... not celebrate?" I asked.

"I mean, traditionally, yes, Christmas has been something I've celebrated."

"But you don't have a tree."

"Correct."

"For how long?"

"I don't know. Probably since my father passed. That was his department."

"But with his passing, wouldn't that task fall to you? You know, so your brother and you could celebrate?"

"Honey, I don't think there is enough spiked eggnog in the world that could make us tolerate each other for a solitary holiday. It was different when we had our father as a buffer. Now, all we would do is bicker."

We were just going to pretend to ignore the fact that he called me 'honey.'

"Yeah... Christmas," I said, throwing up a hand.

"You bicker with your family at Christmas?"

"Well, I won't be this year, but I mean... yeah. There is always little sniping at each other over the meals or old and new traditions or spending too much on gifts. What do you two do for holidays then?"

"Blake throws a Christmas Eve party in the guest house, then sleeps it off most of Christmas Day."

"What about you?"

"It's just another day. I actually get a lot of work done with some overseas countries. You're looking at me like I kicked your puppy."

Okay, he wasn't wrong.

I realized my hand was even over my heart at his words.

"That's just... unacceptable," I declared. "I'm going to be all alone this Christmas, but I am putting up a tree, and baking cookies, and watching Christmas movies."

"You bake?"

"Occasionally, yeah."

"Could I add baking Christmas cookies to your job description?" he asked, looking hopeful.

"What kind of cookies?"

"Any kind of cookies," he decided.

"I can do that. In fact, I will do you one better. I am going to get you a tree too."

"You don't have to do that."

"But if I want to, would you be interested?" I asked.

"I think I might," he agreed, nodding.

"Also, I'm going to make the grounds guy put lights up outside. No one likes a dark, Scrooge house."

To that, I got a smile.

"Okay."

"Anything else I'm missing?" I asked, mostly to myself.

"Christmas music?" Fitz suggested.

"Oh, don't worry. If I am baking, there will be Christmas music blasting. You might regret mentioning it since I sing like a couple of cats engaged in a nasty turf war, but it will be happening."

There was warmth in Fitz's eyes and smile then. So warm, in fact, that it made a gooey sensation move across my chest at the sight of it.

"I'm looking forward to it," he said, and, what's more, I was pretty sure he meant it.

And that, well, it gave me free rein to do something I usually didn't get to do a lot of. Recklessly spending money on Christmas decor. I always picked up one thing here or there, but money was always tight, and I tried to focus more on getting gifts for loved ones than decorations for my house.

But when I'd asked Fitz about the budget for decorating his estate, well, he'd told me to buy whatever I wanted, that the price really didn't matter.

So, yeah, I went a little crazy.

I got a massive tree to suit his tall ceilings, tons of lights and ornaments, garland for the staircase, wreaths for the doors, throw pillows, and little bric-a-brac items to put on sideboards or console tables.

Then I'd bided my time until Fitz had an overnight trip away to get to work. It wasn't nearly as dramatic to watch your house transform into an elegant

Christmas wonderland as it was to walk in to see it decked out.

I worked from morning until late at night the evening he was away crossing the Ts and dotting the Is for his big deal. Then I'd dragged myself out of bed the next morning and got right back at it.

Then, when he still wasn't home, I went ahead and got to work on the cookies with the Christmas music blasting.

It wasn't until I was doing an over-the-top rendition of *All I Want For Christmas Is You* when I turned to find Fitz leaning in the doorway from the garage, watching me with a sweet, bemused expression on his face.

"I, ah, I warned you I couldn't sing," I said, turning down the music. "But it's the enthusiasm that coun—" I started, getting cut off when Fitz pulled away from the doorway, stalked toward me, grabbed me, and sealed his lips to mine.

Fifteen

Fitz

I didn't like being away.

As a creature of habit and comfort, new places, new beds, new sounds and smells, it was all just irritating and off-putting.

I'd been itching to get home.

But I had no idea I would come home to Wynn in my kitchen in a goddamn red sweater dress that was tame by all standards, but managed to hug her curves in just the right ways, baking me what looked like hundreds and hundreds of cookies that were set up all around the counters on drying racks, and belting out a song about wanting someone for Christmas.

It was a gut-punch of feelings watching her as she shimmied her hips and sang as she pulled a baking sheet out of the oven.

I'd lived in this house pretty much my entire life. It never felt quite as much like home as it did with Wynn standing there in my kitchen, making Christmas for me.

I didn't stop to think, to remind myself that I'd decided to play the long game with Wynn since she'd been weirdly skittish since the night of the party.

I'd softened her with the car, I could tell.

And then the way her face lit up when I told her she had full control over decorating? Yeah, I knew I was onto something.

I figured that allowing her to shop and decorate and bake in the house would help her feel less like an employee, and more like someone who had a hand in making a house a home, more like someone who *belonged* there.

I couldn't claim to know what the future held, but I could say that I'd decided I wanted Wynn in it for as long as it suited us both.

The thing I hadn't anticipated, though, was the almost overwhelming sensation of *rightness* when she was in my kitchen like she belonged there, like she would always be there.

It was what ripped away what was left of my control, had me abandoning the long game plan, and storming over to her, grabbing her soft body, and sealing my lips to hers.

There was a moment of stunned inaction before her arms lifted, her hands sliding up my arms, curling around the back of my neck, and pressing her body against mine, melding into me as her lips came alive under mine.

Stepping forward, I backed her up against the island, bending her backward as I deepened the kiss. At her moan, my tongue moved inside to tease over hers as my hands slid from their position at her hips, moving upward to the dip of her waist, up her ribs, then resting at the sides of her breasts until she leaned backward from me, allowing my hands to cover her breasts and squeeze.

Desire made her eyes hazy as she looked at me, her breathing getting faster, ragged, as my thumbs teased over her breasts, but was frustrated by the thick material of her dress and her bra.

Wynn's hand reached for mine, grabbing it, sliding it down over her belly, then up the hem of her skirt. My fingertips teased over the soft skin of her inner thighs before Wynn pressed my hand against the thin strip of material between.

"You're wet for me already," I groaned, feeling her damp panties against my fingers as they started to tease over the sensitive flesh with the barrier for a moment.

"Fitz, please," she moaned, wiggling her hips against me, frustrated, and needing more.

"Please what?" I asked, my thumb teasing around her clit through her panties.

"Please fuck me," she demanded, gaze hungry, ravenous.

I didn't have much control after those words left her lips. I'd managed to keep my hands to myself for what felt like an enviable amount of time, given the fact I knew we both wanted it, were dying for more of what we'd just barely started to explore.

My hand moved up, grabbing a hold of her panties, and yanking until I heard the thin material tearing.

Wynn's eyes went molten at that, but they shut as she moaned when my fingers teased up her drenched pussy without the barrier.

I teased over her clit for an agonizing moment before plunging two fingers inside of her, fucking her with them until she was writhing and panting.

"Fitz... please," she cried, hands clawing at my belt, then my button and zipper. "I need you inside me," she added, reaching into my boxers to pull out my straining cock.

"Turn around," I demanded as I reached for my wallet to find a condom, then slipping it on as Wynn followed instructions, turning around, and pressing her hands to the flour sprinkled counter, arching her ass up toward me, inviting me.

On a growl, my hands grabbed her skirt, yanking it up, exposing her perfect, plump little ass.

Moving forward, I kicked her legs a little wider as I slid my thick cock up her cleft for a moment before grabbing her hip, and slamming inside her.

Hard.

Deep.

And as soon as I was settled inside her, her pussy did that little clenching thing that damn near made me come right then and there.

I had to take a moment to breathe deep before I got control over myself again.

"You're so fucking tight," I groaned as my hips started to rock into her. Not hard or fast, wanting to drive her up more slowly, wanting to hear her crying for release before I gave it to her. "Tell me you've been thinking of me," I demanded. "Here," I added, jerking a little deeper, hearing her breathing hitch at the sensation, then doing it again. "Just like this."

"Y...yes," she moaned, starting to wiggle her hips in circles as I continued to fuck her, trying to get herself closer to the finish line faster than I was going to let her.

"How often?" I demanded, thrusting a little harder.

"All the time," she admitted.

God, I didn't know how badly I needed to hear that until the words were out of her mouth.

I'd never been needy with a woman before. But that was exactly what Wynn made me. Needy. Desperate to know I wasn't the only one feeling the growing connection between us, that she needed me as much as I was starting to need her.

"Are you done fighting this?" I asked, fucking her faster.

"Yes," she whimpered, rocking back into me, getting closer.

"Good," I said, pressing a hand into her back, pushing until she moved flat against the island, her cheek flat on the cold countertop.

Only then did I grab her hips and give her what she needed, what I needed.

I fucked her. Hard and fast and relentless as her pussy got tighter and tighter, as she got closer and closer.

"Come," I demanded as her moans ricocheted off the kitchen walls. "Fuck," I growled as her pussy spasmed around me, as she cried out my name, as she milked my orgasm out of me.

We stayed there for a long moment as we both pulled ourselves back together before I slid out of her, moved away to deal with the condom, and tuck myself away.

By the time I turned back, Wynn was pushing up from the counter, and turning toward me with a big, goofy smile on her face. It took all of two seconds to realize she was completely fucking covered in flour.

"You know, if you wanted me naked, you could have just asked instead of ruining my dress," she told me, patting at the white powder before giving up, reaching down, and pulling the damn thing right off, leaving her standing there in nothing but a barely-there bra.

"That doesn't look like naked to me," I told her, leaning back against the counter because my fucking legs felt weak looking at her.

"What? You don't want to rip this off of me too?" Wynn asked with a saucy little smile as her chin lifted, and her hands went to the clasp between her breasts, undoing it, then sliding the material off, letting it drop carelessly to the floor beside her dress and what was left of her panties. "Better?"

"Infinitely," I agreed, holding out an arm, watching as she fought with herself for a long moment before she gave in and moved forward toward me, letting my arms go around her. "Now, wasn't doing that much better than *not* doing that?" I asked, brow raising as her gaze lowered, masking whatever emotion that may have crossed her eyes.

"Fitz, it's complicated," she insisted as her fingers toyed with the lapel of my jacket.

"What is complicated about it? You want me. I want you. Seems pretty fucking simple."

"Maybe it's that simple for you. But it's not for me."

"Because..." I invited as my fingers drifted up and down her bare back, enjoying the way she shivered at the soft touch.

"Because I work for you," she said, sighing. "If this goes south, your life doesn't change at all. But I would be out of work."

"I wouldn't fire you."

"Sure, you say that now," she said, rolling her eyes. "But if things went bad, like really bad, there is no way you would want me in your house every day still."

"Would you like me to draw up another document about how I will give you a large and comfortable severance package as well as a positive reference should your job no longer exist?" I asked. "I'm not being a smart ass," I added when her gaze cut away again. "If that will make you feel better, I will do that."

"It makes everything sound so business-like."

"It makes it sound like you are being smart and making sure you have your ass covered," I corrected, going ahead and letting my hands glide down to the aforementioned ass, and sinking in.

"You don't think it would be weird for us to be... starting something when I am still working for you?"

"Would you still be doing all your usual daily tasks around the house?"

"Of course."

"Then no. I don't see why one thing has anything to do with the other."

"But..."

"Are you looking for a way out?" I asked. "If you don't want this, that's fine. We move forward like it didn't happen. You just need to say that."

"I'm not saying that," she said. And thank God for that, because I was pretty much just blowing smoke. I wasn't sure it would be possible to move forward like something had never happened between us.

"Good. So, you're just scared," I said, watching as her head shot up, chin lifting defiantly, but I saw the flash of truth in her eyes. "It's okay to be scared. It's new and different. But I feel like it's important to remember that it is new and different for me too. So we can just go ahead and be unsure about shit together. Sound good?"

"I mean, it doesn't sound *good*," she said, rolling her eyes, and getting a choked laugh out of me. "But I think I can be okay with that."

"So," I said, giving her ass another little squeeze. "Now that we have that settled, tell me about these cookies."

"Typical man," she teased, shaking her head. "Thinks with his cock and then his stomach."

"Well, if we want another round or two later, I'm going to need some sustenance."

"What? You're not worried about your waistline?" she teased. "I didn't make you any bland, flavorless cookies to go with the rest of your diet."

"Hey, we've been ordering in," I reminded her, giving her ass a swat.

"True. I'll corrupt you yet," she declared, pulling out of my arms, and moving away from me, giving me a full view of her bare ass as she did so.

"I think you've corrupted me plenty already," I mumbled half to myself, but judging by the way she shot me a sly smirk over her shoulder let me know that she'd absolutely heard me.

So then I ate cookies while Wynn walked around the kitchen bare-ass naked, cleaning up her mess.

Her dress wasn't ruined, of course. She could have slipped it back on at any point. But this was Wynn we were talking about. She liked knowing I was watching. So I didn't even try to conceal the way my eyes watched every movement she made, memorized every curve and freckle of her body as she put away the baking supplies, turned off the oven, and cleaned up the flour we'd managed to get just about everywhere.

I'd eaten about ten cookies by the time she finished.

"What are you doing?" she gasped when I moved up behind her as she was putting bowls back into a high cabinet, going up on her very tiptoes to reach.

I lowered myself down to my knees as I pressed her legs further apart.

"I'm still hungry."

Sixteen

Wynn

If at any point I'd been worried that Fitz and my chemistry might fizzle out once we'd had sex a few times, it all disappeared as I moved around his kitchen wearing nothing but my shoes, putting away supplies as Fitz stood there watching me.

I always figured the thrill was in them never knowing that I knew I was being watched.

But, as it turned out, even just having the one man I wanted above all others eye-fucking me from across the room was enough to have me achy and needy even after he'd already given me an intense orgasm.

Then, oh, then, when he'd stormed across the room, dropped down behind me, told me he was hungry, then ate me better and longer than anyone before in my entire life, sending me through three solid orgasms until my legs refused to hold me anymore? Yeah, I was pretty sure things would never get dull between us then.

When I'd finally managed to shake some life back into my legs, I'd taken his hand and led him out into the rest of the house.

I won't lie, I got an immense amount of pleasure from watching him take in all the work I'd done to transform the house.

"Wow, honey," he said, spinning me back to face him. "Just... wow," he added, pulling me close, and sealing his lips to mine.

It was a slow, lingering kiss.

Even so, though, I could feel the stirrings of something less sweet inside me. And I could feel the way Fitz's cock was pressing against me again by the time he'd kissed my lips swollen and tender.

Reaching down, I grabbed his cock through his pants, stroking him as his gaze got hotter and hotter.

"Wynn..." he growled as I worked his cock free, then started to undo the buttons of his shirt, wanting to finally get more of him.

"Hmm?" I asked, my fingers dancing up the bare skin of his stomach and chest before snagging his shirt and jacket, and sliding them off his shoulders.

"Aren't you tired?"

"Of you? Not yet," I said, shooting him a smirk as my hands pushed his pants and boxers off his hips.

He was still kicking out of his shoes as I lowered myself down in front of him, looking up at him for a long moment before running my tongue up the underside of his cock before sucking him into my mouth.

There was something magnificent about him right then. This larger-than-life, powerful, beautiful man looking down at me with hunger and need in his eyes. Hunger and need that I'd put there.

I wanted to watch him, but it wasn't long before his hand was grabbing the back of my neck, making me take him deeper and harder and faster, making it impossible to see as he fucked my mouth until he was groaning and hissing out his breath.

"Enough," he growled, yanking me away, then lowering down onto the floor with me, pushing me down onto my back on his discarded shirt and jacket as he fished another condom out of his wallet and slipped it on.

His hands went out, grabbing my legs, yanking them up, and resting my ankles on his shoulder before he surged inside me.

Crossing my ankles, I felt him more intensely even as he pressed a hand on my lower stomach, increasing the pressure, making me acutely aware of each thick inch as he started to fuck me. A little slower at first, taking his time, making me writhe and moan and beg him for release.

"No," he growled, quickly slipping out of me just as I felt an orgasm start to crest, leaving me rolling onto my side and groaning at the denial of it. "Not yet," he told me, dropping down next to me, and pulling me up to straddle him. "Come here," he demanded, grabbing the back of my neck, pulling me down for a kiss even as he grabbed his cock, sliding it up and down my slick cleft, but making sure he avoided direct contact with my clit, wanting me panting and whimpering, but unable to get close to that release my body was screaming for.

"Fitz, please," I moaned, my hips wiggling, needing him inside me again, but this time with me in control.

Fitz slid his cock down, pressing against the entrance of my body, waiting until I pushed upright, and lowered myself down on him with a sigh.

"Beautiful," he said, his hand sliding up my thigh, over my hip, my ribs, then teasing over my breast as I started to ride him. Slow at first—up and down, but getting faster as my hips started to go in circles, feeling his thickness hit my walls as I leaned back slightly, bracing my hands on his bent legs to engage my G-spot.

Fitz watched me as I rode him, his eyes molten, his jaw tight with his own growing need for release that had him thrusting his hips upward into me fast even as my hips continued to circle, pushing me closer and closer to oblivion.

His free hand moved between my thighs again as my pussy tightened around him, started to work my clit with slow, lazy movements.

Maybe that should have been my sign.

But I was too far gone to think straight.

That is until I felt that first beginning spasm.

And Fitz suddenly grabbed my hips, lifting me up and off of him, once again denying my release.

The need was an acute, painful thing then, leaving my body feeling shaky and foreign to me even as Fitz got back onto his knees, and pulled me in for another kiss.

Hard, almost bruising for a moment.

And then he was grabbing me again, turning me, and pressing me down on all fours as he moved in behind me, massaging, then slapping my ass, the sound echoing around the walls and high ceilings of the entryway.

I would have enjoyed the sound, but then he was thrusting inside me, stealing away all my thoughts but the feeling of him as he started to fuck me.

Hard.

Fast.

Determined.

Like maybe, just maybe, he was going to let me come this time.

I dropped my lower back down, creating the perfect angle for him to push me right to that edge.

I was teetering there when I became aware of a sound. Footsteps. And a voice. Female. And it was calling my name as it got closer and closer.

As recognition hit, as she moved into the foyer, it was too late.

Too late to react.

Too late to stop the orgasm that slammed through my system.

I was crashing even as Perry seemed to realize what she'd just walked in on.

Her eyes were huge as Fitz slammed deep inside me, growling out my name as he came with me.

"Sorry! Sorry!" she squeaked, turning, and rushing away even as the waves pulled me under one last time before I could even pull in a breath again, let alone think straight.

"Oh my God. Oh my God. Oh my *God*," I hissed, pulling away from Fitz, and dropping down on my ass, cradling my face in my hands.

"Yeah... wasn't expecting that," Fitz agreed, wincing at me.

I mean, Perry and I were close. Super close. Had seen each other naked on more than one occasion close.

But it didn't matter how close you were with your friends, they typically didn't expect to walk in on you getting railed by your—and their former—boss.

Yes, I liked being watched.

But just... you know... not by my loved ones.

I was freaking *mortified*.

"You should go try to talk to her," Fitz suggested, giving my shoulder a reassuring squeeze.

"And say what?" I asked, shaking my head. "*Hey, sorry you walked in on me getting fucked from behind by my boss?*"

"I thought we agreed I'm not just your boss anymore," Fitz said.

"You being more than my boss doesn't make this less embarrassing. I was literally coming as she walked in," I added, voice choked.

"I'm sure Perry isn't the first person in the world to happen upon her best friend having sex. She is a grown woman. She will get over it. Go see if you can catch her and talk it out," he urged.

I knew he was right.

Perry and I could talk anything out.

I mean, I'd once talked her through finding a tampon she'd lost inside herself from just the other side of the bathroom door.

She'd given me all the details on the first time she'd tried anal.

We could get past this.

But he was right, the sooner the better.

"I can't," I declared, looking over at him.

"Why not?"

"Because my dress is in the kitchen," I said, letting out a pained laugh.

"Take my shirt," Fitz suggested, climbing off of it, and holding it out to me so I could slip my arms in.

I buttoned up fast before looking back at him.

"Go, honey," he demanded, giving me a gentle shove.

And then I was running.

"Perry!" I called, rushing down the hall toward the kitchen where she must have come in like she would have when she worked there. "Perry!" I called, louder.

"Right here," Perry called back.

I moved into the kitchen to find her half out the door to the garage, her gaze on her feet even as I moved into the room.

"I, ah, should have noticed the pile of discarded clothes on the floor," she admitted, waving toward my dress, bra, and torn panties. "I was excited. I just... I wasn't noticing anything. I'm so sorry. I didn't mean to, you know, walk in on you."

"I'm sorry too," I said, still feeling how heated my cheeks felt. "I never meant for you to see that," I added.

"Or tell me it was going on?" Perry asked, tone as accusatory as her gaze as mine found hers.

"That's... that's a sort of long story," I admitted.

"I thought we didn't keep secrets. Not even sex secrets."

To be fair, she was the one who didn't seem to keep any.

But she was right.

I would usually at least tell her if I was getting physical with someone, even if I left out the details.

"I know," I agreed. "It's just... okay, do you really want to know?" I asked.

"God, when you say it like that, I'm not sure," she said, wincing, but then giving me a smile. "Of course I want to know. You're banging a billionaire," she added in a small voice from behind a raised hand like she was sharing a bit of town gossip in church.

"I know, right?" I said, going toward the wine rack, and finding the bottle that seemed to be the least expensive, waving it at Perry.

"I think we might need that," she agreed, nodding.

I opened and poured, gave her a glass, and then we both took a long sip before I broke the silence.

"Okay. I am just going to throw it all out there. I have this... fetish," I admitted.

"For billionaires?" she asked, smile devilish.

"For being watched," I admitted.

There was a moment of surprise before she rolled her eyes. "Oh, for God's sake. No wonder you were so curious about the cameras!"

"Yeahhhh," I said, taking another sip for courage.

"So, you took this job because you wanted him to, you know, watch you on the cameras? Doing what? Chores?"

"Ah, sort of," I admitted. "At first. Just doing chores. But in short skirts or low-cut blouses."

"You little slut," she teased, beaming at me.

"I know, right?"

"But... it became more than that, obviously."

"It shouldn't have," I admitted. "I don't usually want to sleep with someone when they've been watching me. It takes the thrill away.

"But Fitzwilliam Buchanan ended up being... thrilling?"

"I'm sort of seeing him, so you can probably just call him Fitz now," I said.

"He will forever be Fitzwilliam Buchanan to me," Perry declared. "But, yay, right? We're happy about this?"

"It's...it's very new. I mean, the part where we decided to be more than boss and employee with a sprinkling of voyeurism. It's very new. But I am... tentatively happy?" I said, shrugging.

"How about just being happy-happy? You deserve that."

"I guess. It just all feels like a whirlwind."

"It has been, but what's wrong with that? Sometimes, things just click."

"I guess," I agreed. "And he's been really nice to me. He got me a new car. With not only butt warmers, but a heated steering wheel and armrests too."

"Marry him," Perry said, not a fan of winter like I was, so she appreciated anything that kept her warmer.

"What were you doing here?" I asked, topping off her wine. "You never come here."

"I know. I just... I just got the call."

"The call for wh—oh, did you hear back from the soap?" I asked, excitement building.

"Yes! I got it. I like... got it got it. Like they want me for at least a full season. And I will be part of the main cast. I have this love triangle thing going on with two of the hottest guys on the show."

"Oh, Perry. I am so happy for you. You so deserve this," I said, putting down my glass, and wrapping my arms around her, actually feeling tears flood my eyes, knowing how hard she'd worked to get something serious going for herself.

"I had to come and tell you in person. I almost can't believe it," she admitted as I pulled back, grabbing my glass, this time to toast her.

"I can. You're phenomenal. It was only a matter of time before someone saw that, and had to have you. Cheers to this amazing new opportunity!" I said, clinking my glass to hers.

"It's kind of the perfect role for me," she admitted. "She's an over-the-top, dramatic, emotional girl who doesn't know what is good for her where love is concerned. And, well, there's this other thing..."

"What other thing?" I asked, noticing the way her cheeks went as pink as mine had been before.

"Well, since we are sharing our deepest, dirtiest secrets tonight," she said with an eyebrow wiggle at my expense, before she went back to seeming wholly uncomfortable with whatever she was about to admit to me. "You know how I said the role was for a character in a sort of love triangle?"

"Yes."

"Well, see, you like being watched. I, ah, I like... being... shared," she admitted, barely able to choke the words out.

"No way!" I said, smile huge. "Like at once?"

"Like separate sometimes, but also at once sometimes too."

"You little slut, you," I teased. "I love that for you."

"I know, right? Art imitates life in this case, I guess."

"I feel so much closer to you right now," I admitted. "And not just because you've now witnessed me making the beast with two backs," I added.

"That's what makes what I am about to say so much worse."

"What?" I asked, heart sinking.

"I have to move to L.A.," she told me, and the fact was a knife to the gut even as I tried to remind myself that she was having all her dreams come true there.

"Oh," I said, taking a deep breath, then a sip of my wine. "Well, luckily for us, I am dating a billionaire who can like... charter a plane for me to come to brunch with you anytime I want," I said, watching as some of the tension left her shoulders.

"That's true. And when I come visit, I can take a bath in that tub I've fantasized about."

"That tub is as good as you've imagined," I told her.

"I'd have to insist that the cameras be moved first, though," she said, reaching for a cookie. "Did you ever find out what the cameras were about?" she asked, shaking her head. "Or is he just into... watching?"

"I mean, he was. When I put on a show for him. But I don't think he knew he was into that sort of thing until I showed it to him. I actually have no idea what the cameras are about," I admitted, frowning a bit at that realization.

"You have to ask," she insisted.

"No, I totally do," I agreed.

"He's really kind of a treat to look at, isn't he?" she asked, shooting me a familiar smile.

"He's a whole feast to look at," I shot back. "And he handed me a credit card and told me I could make it look like Christmas threw up all over the house. He wasn't going to celebrate at all."

"That's so sad," Perry said, pressing her hand to her heart, my dear, dramatic friend.

"I know, right?" I agreed.

"Will you be spending the holiday with him now? I was feeling so bad about going home to see my family."

"I guess we will spend it together. He probably hasn't had a holiday meal in years."

"I love watching you be a little homemaker."

"I'm kind of enjoying it a lot too."

"This house could use to feel more like a home."

"I agree. It needs some warming up. Starting with the hideous art he has everywhere."

"Oh, it would be so amazing to see some of your art up in here. Maybe one of the new pieces? What— oh," she said when I took a guilty sip of my wine. "Ohhh, are the new pieces dirty?" she asked, knowing me far too well.

"Some more so than others," I agreed.

"Well, now that I have seen the art... in action," she said, laughing at my pained groan, "can I see the actual art pieces?"

"Okay. Maybe some of them. Some I think are for my eyes only," I said.

"What is for your eyes only?" Fitz asked, coming into the kitchen wearing a pair of lightweight black pajama pants and a white tee. It was the most casual I'd ever seen him dressed. Which, somehow, felt almost as intimate as having him naked with me.

"Oh, the canvases she's done heavily featuring, I imagine, your penis," Perry declared, surprising Fitz enough to make him pause mid-stride and turn a choking noise into a cough.

"She's not wrong," I admitted, shrugging at him.

"You've been painting me?" he asked, sounding both flabbergasted and touched at the same time.

"I had to work out my feelings for you somehow," I told him.

"And instead of talking it out with me, you painted it."

"Yes, like the totally normal, not at all emotionally insecure artist that she is," Perry agreed, getting small eyes from me.

"Perry, nice to see you again," Fitz said, offering her a small smile, not at all bothered by the fact that she'd seen us fucking. But, then again, she wasn't his best friend.

"You too. Thanks for the wine," she said, toasting him.

"I tried to pick out the least expensive-looking bottle," I admitted, waving toward it.

"And somehow managed to choose the most expensive," he said with a chuckle as he reached for my glass, taking it for a sip.

"Well, she's worth it, at least," Perry declared, always ready to jump to my defense, and I loved her all the more in that moment.

"That she is," Fitz agreed, wrapping an arm around my lower back, fingers digging in at my waist. Firm, possessive.

He got the smile of approval from Perry at those words.

"So, Fitzwilliam," Perry started.

"Fitz," he corrected.

"Mr. Buchanan," Perry tried again.

"When she would talk about you when she worked here, she called you by your full name. Like you were a celebrity or something," I informed him.

"Anyway," Perry said, rolling her eyes. "While I am over the moon that you and my best friend here have a shared interest in her exhibitionism, we have a question for you."

"Uh oh," Fitz mumbled, taking another sip of my drink. "What's that?"

"What's with all the cameras?" she blurted out, making his body tense a bit.

"Oh, right," he said, looking uncomfortable.

"I mean, you know it is totally not normal to have them all over your house like this, right? It's why I quit."

"You knew they were there?" Fitz asked, brows pinching.

"Of course I knew. I used to nanny. Hidden cameras aren't all that hidden if you know what you're looking for. What?" she asked, making me turn my head to look at Fitz who looked like he'd just been kicked in the gut.

"What's wrong? Is it about the cameras?" I asked.

"Yes. Sort of."

"Why do you have them?"

"Because someone has been stealing from me," Fitz explained.

"What? Really?" I asked. "Who do you think it is?"

"I think it's Blake," Fitz admitted, and suddenly, all the animosity he felt toward his brother made a lot of sense. If I offered my fancy guest house and a job and an allowance to someone who returned the favor by stealing from me, I would have a hard time carrying on any civil conversations with them as well.

"Really? Blake?" I asked.

"What? You don't think so?" he asked.

"I don't know. I mean, I guess he is capable. But Blake strikes me more like someone who would steal from you blatantly, don't you think? Just grab something off your shelf as he was walking away, in full sight of you."

"You're not wrong," Fitz admitted. "He likes to push buttons almost as much as he likes money."

"And you do have a lot of people in and out of the house on a weekly basis," I added. There was always something getting maintenance or serviced or projects getting done.

"True," Fitz agreed. "So, it could be anyone."

"Pretty much," I agreed, giving him a wince. "Has the stealing stopped since the cameras were installed?"

"No. That's the frustrating part. The cameras have been up for almost a year, but shit is still going missing. I can't figure it out. Well, no, that's not true. Things haven't gone missing in a few months."

"I didn't steal anything!" Perry squeaked, thinking he was going to blame her. "I mean, I totally stole some apples and oranges. But you always made me order too many, and they would go bad before you ate them."

"Yeah, hon, I'm not talking about apples and oranges. Art and electronics have been going missing. Up until..." he said, looking at me.

"Until I started?" I asked. "Really?"

"Yeah..."

"Well, I have an answer for that," Perry said. "I was a terrible house manager," she declared.

"I noticed that," Fitz agreed with a smile because he seemed to sense that Perry wasn't the sort to get offended by him agreeing with her.

"I spent way more time than I should have taking selfies or phone calls between tasks. Whoever is stealing could have seized the opportunities in those moments to snatch something."

"Yes, but how?" Fitz asked. "I have cameras damn near everywhere."

"Maybe they're like me. They know they're there."

"But they should have been in the camera's view several times with what has gone missing."

"I'm no security camera expert, but I'm pretty sure you can find a dozen different ways to trick a camera online if you are looking to do it," Perry suggested. "And they were smooth sailing with house managers the likes of me around who shirked responsibilities. But then Wynn came along, all Type A and dedicated to her work, and she stole their windows of opportunity."

"It's not a bad theory," I agreed, nodding.

"I agree. But how the hell am I supposed to figure out who it is then?"

"Those little tracking devices on or in expensive items?" Perry suggested. "Or some extra cameras. Then give Wynn off for a few days. Paid, of course," she added, shooting me a wink.

"Of course," Fitz agreed.

"So, what I am hearing is I can trust you to keep my best friend's interest at heart while I run off to be a big daytime TV star."

"You can. And congratulations."

"Thank you," she said, giving him one of her warm smiles. "So, you're rich."

"I, ah, yes," Fitz agreed, a little uncomfortable with her bluntness.

"So, when I happen to have a free afternoon, you can fly her out to me no problem."

"I, yeah, I can do that," Fitz agreed, giving me a squeeze.

"I mean, you can visit too. So long as we get some time to eat pasta on the couch and rewatch things we've seen a million times."

"I think I can manage that."

"Good. Then it's settled. I approve of this relationship," Perry declared, clinking my glass with hers. She took a sip before putting her glass down. "Okay. Well. On that note, I have a boyfriend to break-up with. And I know, I know," she said looking at me. "I can see the 'Thank God' all over your face. Oh, and call my family. And start packing my things. And..."

"Packing party. After Christmas," I demanded.

"Yes, absolutely. You bring the wine," she said, shooting a smirk to Fitz. "Another bottle of the *cheap* stuff, maybe."

And with that, she was gone as suddenly as she had arrived, leaving Fitz and me alone again.

He reached for a coffee.

I got more wine.

"Are you upset?" he asked after downing a whole and a half chocolate chip cookie.

"That she's leaving? A little, yeah. I mean, I am going to miss her like crazy. But I'm so happy for her. She's worked hard for this. And she's going to do great."

"You're a good friend."

"So is she," I agreed.

Fitz finished his cookie, took a sip from my glass, then set it down and reached for me, sealing his lips to mine, mixing the taste of the red wine and the chocolate in the cookies.

"Want to go upstairs?" he asked, eyes heated.

"You can't possibly have any strength left," I said, smiling up at him.

"Not really," he admitted. "Which is why you are going to ride my face, then ride my cock, and then we are both going to catch some sleep before we repeat the process all over again. Sound good?"

"Perfect," I corrected.

It sounded perfect.

Seventeen

Fitz

"Get out of that water right now and fuck me," Wynn demanded as I surfaced for some air after almost finishing my laps for the day.

I'd needed to add ten more laps since Wynn had become a staple in my life. Well, Wynn and her fast food addiction and snacking habit. Which meant I was eating a lot more crap than usual.

Doubly so since I'd needed to fire Elsbeth, my cook that I'd had for years who made all of my—as Wynn would put it—"bland" meals.

See, I'd done what Perry had suggested with tracking devices and new cameras, then I'd given Wynn some time off.

And, sure enough, the new camera caught her red-handed, stealing some vase my father had brought into the house before his death.

According to Elsbeth, she and my father had been involved in some lengthy affair, and she'd felt slighted when he'd left her nothing in the will.

I doubted that story and fired her, but chose not to press charges.

Call it the Christmas spirit.

But Christmas had come and gone.

We'd spent the morning in bed before going down and surprising each other with gifts, then I got to watch—since she refused to let me help—as she made us Christmas dinner.

Then, trying to mend half-burnt bridges, she'd even invited Blake over for dinner.

We'd eaten and talked and then watched a movie.

And it had been pleasant.

No arguing, no hurt feelings, just a group of people enjoying a holiday together like we were supposed to.

Eventually, Blake had taken off to finish sleeping off the party from the night before, and Wynn and I had snuggled on the couch watching Christmas movies.

We'd stuffed our faces with cookies then headed upstairs where we'd made slow, sweet love until we were both spent.

It had been the best holiday of my life.

And I knew as I held her while she drifted off that I wanted a lifetime of Christmases just like that one. Though, eventually, we'd throw some kids into the mix too.

"Wynn..." I said, shaking my head even as she yanked down her bathing suit bottoms, and slid into the water. "Oh," I said, smiling at her as she swam over to me, wrapping me up with arms and legs, and trailing kisses up my neck, attempting—and succeeding—to get me hard. "The pool guy just pulled in, didn't he?" I asked as she reached down into my shorts, pulling out my cock and stroking it until it was straining.

"Yes, and you need to fuck me before he gets here and sees what we're doing," she said, a wicked glint in her eyes as her thighs grabbed my sides as she lifted her body upward, and slid down on my cock.

Her hot, tight pussy was such a change from the cold water that a shiver racked through me at the sensation.

Wynn's arms went around my neck, her forearms braced on my shoulders for stability as she started to lift up, then drop back down. Slow and measured since she didn't have much leverage.

"Unless, of course, you want him to watch us fuck," she added, eyes already getting heavy-lidded. "I'd be okay with that too."

On a groan, I slammed her back against the wall of the pool, pistoning inside her. Fast, deep, driving her up hard and fast.

I didn't give a fuck if the pool guy caught me fucking Wynn. There was even a small thrill at the idea of him seeing, a hidden sort of desire I never would have known about if not for Wynn.

But once my cock was inside her, I needed a release just as badly as she needed the thrill of maybe being seen, being watched.

"Harder, Fitz," she begged as her nails scratched my back bloody as her pussy tightened around me. "Fuck, yes, just like that," she cried between her moans that echoed loudly off the walls in the room. "Don't stop," she cried, her legs starting to shake.

"You're so fucking tight," I growled, fucking her harder still, spurred on by her loud moans, her filthy demands as she got closer and closer. "Fuck," I hissed as her pussy clamped my cock harder as she got right to that edge. "Come for me," I demanded, voice rough. "Let me feel you squeeze my cock," I told her.

And just like that, she was crying out my name as she came.

I fucked her through it, wanting to drag it out.

But before I could slam deep and find my own release, she was all but leaping off of me, then dropping low in the water, and opening her mouth wide.

I didn't need more than that.

I slipped my cock between her lips and fucked her mouth until the climax was slamming through me, making me shove my cock deep into her throat, and coming so hard I was fucking blinded by it for a moment.

"Shit," a third-party voice hissed, making my eyes shoot open, looking down at Wynn who, with my cock still dripping down her throat, attempted to shoot me a smile at the fact that we'd been caught. "Sorry.

Sorry," the guy said again, and there was a crashing noise as he rushed out of the pool room.

"You," I said, shaking my head at her as I pulled my cock out of her mouth.

"I know. I'm a dirty little slut, huh?" she asked, eyes triumphant.

My hand reached out, my thumb gliding across her lower lip.

"But you're *my* dirty little slut," I agreed, feeling that familiar warming sensation across my chest. I got it every time I was close to her, but especially anytime one of us referred to her as mine.

Because that was what she was.

Mine.

I had a ring waiting in my study drawer to seal the deal.

I was just waiting for the right time.

I knew when it was, too.

The night of her art exhibit.

The same art exhibit I'd arranged for her as a Christmas present.

"That's true," she agreed, moving to stand again, wrapping her arms around my neck. "Do you think we traumatized the pool man?" she asked, looking pleased at the prospect.

"I think he's probably out jerking off in his truck," I corrected.

"Yeah?" she asked, eyes heated again because she got off on having that kind of power.

"Yep," I agreed. There was no way I could have walked in on some beautiful woman getting throat-fucked without ending up with a hard-on either.

"Hmm," she said.

"Woman, I need some recovery time," I told her, recognizing that light in her eye.

"What? About an hour or two, you think?" she asked, eyes dancing. "I could get some painting done," she declared. "And by then, the guys should be here to put down the mulch," she told me, beaming at the idea.

I needed to get some work done.

And I did.

For about an hour and a half while Wynn painted.

But then she was barreling into my study, grabbing my hand, and dragging me upstairs and into our bedroom, pushing me onto the bed, and doing a striptease that turned into a lap dance that, despite my certainty that I needed more time, made my cock rock fucking hard in a moment.

"Come on," she demanded, pulling me forward with her, turning her ass toward me. "Fuck me against the window," she added, wiggling her ass against me until my cock pressed against her wet cleft.

My gaze moved over her shoulder to see the guys moving around, gathering their wheelbarrows and shovels and landscaping tarp. Busy. They were all busy with their task.

It didn't matter to us if they actually saw, but that there was a chance for it.

My balls felt ready to burst at the idea as my cock surged inside her.

"He's looking," Wynn groaned out as I started to fuck her harder, her whole body jolting each time I thrust inside her.

"Let him," I growled. The whole world could watch me fuck her if they wanted. She was mine. No one else was going to touch her. They could all go green with envy for all I cared.

"I'm..." Wynn choked out even as her pussy started to clench my cock, dragging me through my orgasm too.

I yanked her backward with me, collapsing back onto the bed with her sprawled over me, her back to my chest.

"This is never going to get old," she declared after a long moment.

"No, it's not," I agreed. "But you need to go get to work on your pieces for the exhibit," I reminded her.

"I'm suddenly feeling very inspired," she told me.

"We talked about this. No cock canvases," I reminded her, walking my fingers across her stomach.

"Those are for our private gallery only," she confirmed, rolling onto her stomach, and smiling down at me. "How about while I work, you order in something greasy and fatty?" she suggested. "Then when I finish, we can eat and watch Perry's soap."

"I'll never forgive you for getting me hooked on that show," I griped, like I'd been griping for weeks, since Perry finally made an appearance.

"Oh, you love every second of it, and you know it."

"I still feel like she has a freaky amount of chemistry with those two male leads of hers. What?" I asked when a mischievous smile toyed at her lips.

"Nothing. Nothing at all."

"Best friend stuff," I assumed.

"Exactly. You will have to compliment her the next time you talk to her. I still have to call her about the exhibit. Speaking of, did I thank you for setting that up yet?"

"Not in the last... thirty minutes."

"Well, thank you," she said, sealing her lips to mine.

"You're welcome," I said as she slid off of me and walked bare-ass naked out of the bedroom, across the hallway over the foyer, and into her studio she'd set up in one of the spare rooms.

When she emerged a few hours later with paint staining various parts of her bare skin, curling up with me on the couch eating Chinese and watching an over-the-top soap opera, I was overcome with the rightness of it all.

I was one lucky fucking man.

Epilogue

Wynn

I was the luckiest woman in the world.
And I wasn't even being dramatic.
That was the best part.
I wasn't the girl I used to be, the one who
feasted on the scraps men offered me and then boasted
about the meal he'd given to me to friends and family.
No.

Fitz laid out a spread for me that would feed me for months, for decades, for the rest of my life.

For a man who was accustomed to being on his own, with really only himself—and Blake's mishaps—to worry about, he'd been surprisingly adept at starting and growing a relationship.

The man had somehow managed to get me an exhibit for a Christmas present, for goodness sakes.

Which was where we were.

I'd dreamed of my first exhibit a million times over the years. But none of those daydreams came anything close to the reality.

Fitz had gotten me in at an intimate gallery with their trademarked floor-to-ceiling front windows and white walls so foot traffic would see the art, and possibly decide to head inside to buy something.

And I got the whole damn thing to myself. No sharing wall space. I got to fill as much of it as I wanted.

Admittedly, I'd gone a little crazy. But, despite usually hearing only positive things about my art, there was still that insecure little artist inside of me that was sure people were going to drag her through the mud.

So I'd filled the place with all different styles from landscapes to portraits and everything in between.

The crowd was amazing, too. Between my old art school buddies and Fitz's friends, it had been pretty much packed since the doors opened.

Fitz was standing with my parents looking at a portrait I'd done of my mom walking in her garden in a flowing tan dress, her hair kicking up in the breeze, her arm extended, running her fingers over the faces of the wildflowers she'd planted many years before.

It was one of my favorites.

Enough so that I'd painted it twice.

One to sell, one to keep.

"Can I steal Fitz for just one minute?" I asked, linking my arm through his.

"Of course you can, honey," my mom said, giving me a big smile.

"What's going on?" Fitz asked, brows pinching as I led him toward the back of the gallery.

"I have a painting that I did just for you," I told him, barely able to contain my amusement, my little joke that I hoped would be as funny to him as it was to me.

"You did?" he asked, sounding touched. "Wait, Wynn," he said, eyes going big.

"It's not a cock canvas, don't worry," I told him, leaning my head against his arm. "Here," I said, breaking away to move a carefully positioned fake plant out of the way.

And there it was.

My gift to him.

A big, ugly white canvas with a few black and gray streaks across it.

"In homage to your terrible taste in art before you met me," I said as he stared at it for a second before he burst out laughing.

I thought nothing of him reaching into his pocket.

But then he was lowering himself down on one knee.

And opening the little blue box in his hand.

Then there it was.

The perfect ring.

Not a plain clear diamond cut in a circle or a square, a stone and a style that wouldn't have suited me at all.

No.

It was a big ol' pear-cut yellow diamond lined with little pink diamonds.

Over the top, colorful, and unique.

Perfect.

It was absolutely perfect.

"Oh my God," I gasped, my gaze slipping from the ring to his lovely face. The face of the man who was making all my dreams—ones I'd known all my life, and ones that I was just starting to realize—come to life.

"Marry me, Wynn," he said, voice low even as the gasps and *Awwws* from the crowd started as they realized what was happening.

Was it still a relatively new relationship?

Yes.

But had I known almost since the moment we'd finally gotten together that it was something different, something special?

Absolutely.

"Yes," I said, sticking my hand out toward him.

He grabbed the ring and slipped it on my finger.

Once it was on, I reached out, grabbing his face, leaning forward, and sealing my lips to his.

Fitz got to his feet, wrapping his arms around me, and deepening the kiss.

We broke apart to applause, and even as my mom rushed forward, a familiar voice rose above the other noise in the room.

"Yay! I didn't miss it!" Perry squealed, running through the crowd, and throwing herself at the both of us.

"Per!" I said, squeezing her back with one arm, my other one still around Fitz. "You came!"

"Of course I came. I was going to come just for the exhibit because it is a huge deal, but then your man here told me it was going to be an extra special event, and sent me a ticket to fly out. First class ticket, I might add. It was a fancy flight," she said, giving Fitz a big smile. "He's a keeper," she declared.

"I'm keeping him," I agreed, showing her the ring.

"Oh, it's as perfect as he said it was," she said, huge smile on her face.

"It is," I agreed. "So how are you?"

"Good! I am loving the warmth out in L.A. And the people. They're all as dramatic as I am," she said with a smirk that said she knew she was over-the-top a lot of the time. "And the show is fantastic."

"You have a lot of chemistry with both those guys," Fitz said, being my fellow soap opera addict.

Perry's gaze slid to mine, a light in her eyes that was unmistakable.

Yes, Perry liked being shared.

And something was telling me that her on-screen triangle was, in fact, a real-life three-way relationship of some sort.

"I'm so happy for you," I told her, reaching out to give her hand a squeeze.

"I'm so happy for you too. Oh, except for this," she said, looking past me at the piece I'd done for Fitz as a joke. "What the hell is this?" she asked.

The rest of the night was a blur of congratulations and seeing little red stickers appearing in the corners of canvases that had found buyers.

"Oh, you didn't," I said as Fitz pulled me outside afterward, and a limo pulled up.

"Oh, I did," he said, voice husky because he already knew what I had in mind. And it involved nudity and a raised partition. "I also got us a hotel room that has floor-to-ceiling windows on two sides," he added, leaning down to nibble my ear.

Did I mention he was the perfect man?

Because he was.

And he was all mine.

And we would have a whole lifetime to find ways to *accidentally* be caught doing naughty things...

Also by Jessica Gadziala

If you liked this book, check out these other series and titles in the NAVESINK BANK UNIVERSE:

Navesink Bank Henchmen MC
Reign
Cash
Wolf
Repo
Duke
Renny
Lazarus

Pagan
Cyrus
Edison
Reeve
Sugar
The Fall of V
Adler
Roderick
Virgin
Roan
Camden
West
Colson

Henchmen MC Next Gen
Niro
Malcolm
Fallon

The Savages
Monster
Killer
Savior

Mallick Brothers
For A Good Time, Call
Shane
Ryan
Mark
Eli
Charlie & Helen: Back to the Beginning

Investigators
367 Days
14 Weeks
4 Months

Dark
Dark Mysteries
Dark Secrets
Dark Horse

Professionals
The Fixer
The Ghost
The Messenger
The General
The Babysitter
The Middle Man
The Negotiator
The Client
The Cleaner

Rivers Brothers
Lift You Up
Lock You Down
Pull You In

Grassi Family
The Woman at the Docks
The Women in the Scope

Golden Glades Henchmen MC
Huck
Che
McCoy

STANDALONES WITHIN NAVESINK BANK:

Vigilante
Grudge Match

NAVESINK BANK LEGACY SERIES:

The Rise of Ferryn
Counterfeit Love

<u>OTHER SERIES AND STANDALONES:</u>

Stars Landing

What The Heart Needs
What The Heart Wants
What The Heart Finds
What The Heart Knows
The Stars Landing Deviant
What The Heart Learns

Surrogate

The Sex Surrogate
Dr. Chase Hudson

The Green Series

Into the Green
Escape from the Green

Seven Sins MC

The Sacrifice
The Healer
The Thrall

Costa Family

The Woman in the Trunk

The Woman in the Back Room

DEBT

Dissent

Stuffed: A Thanksgiving Romance

Unwrapped

Peace, Love, & Macarons

A Navesink Bank Christmas

Don't Come

Fix It Up

N.Y.E.

faire l'amour

Revenge

There Better Be Pie

I Like Being Watched

About the Author

Jessica Gadziala is a full-time writer, parrot enthusiast, and coffee drinker who has an unhealthy obsession with acquiring houseplants. She enjoys short rides to the book store, sad songs, and cold weather. She lives in New Jersey with her parrots, dogs, bunnies, and a whole flock of chickens.

She is very active on Goodreads, Facebook, as well as her personal groups on those sites. Join in. She's friendly.

Stalk Her!

Connect with Jessica:

Facebook:
https://www.facebook.com/JessicaGadziala/
Facebook Group:
https://www.facebook.com/groups/314540025563403/

Goodreads:
https://www.goodreads.com/author/show/13800950.Jessica_Gadziala
Goodreads Group:
https://www.goodreads.com/group/show/177944-jessica-gadziala-books-and-bullsh

Twitter: @JessicaGadziala

Website: JessicaGadziala.com

Amazon: https://www.amazon.com/Jessica-Gadziala/e/B00VRU7IOS/ref=dp_byline_cont_pop_ebooks_1

TikTok
Instagram

<3/ Jessica

9 798468 478936